DEDICATION

To my Brickies

Words cannot express how much I appreciate every last one of you. You've made this journey of unpredictability fun, uplifting, and one hundred-percent worth the ride. Thanks for your never-ending support. I promise to keep giving you the best that I've got, Anita Baker style!

To my Brickie Beta Squad

For always answering the call. For always stepping up hungry for these lil ole words of mine. For your love, your support, and your always valuable feedback, thank you from the bottom of my beating heart!

SYNOPSIS

Some of life's greatest lessons are learned by trial and error.

Fall enough times, you'll learn how to walk.

Bite your tongue enough times, you'll learn to speak up.

Lose enough times, you'll learn how to win.

Get burnt enough times, you'll learn how to avoid the flame.

But what happens when two tormented souls suffer too many losses? Is it enough for fate to bring them together and let them to do the rest? Or will they find it impossible to learn *how to love*?

One

Jo

My hair was all over my head, spread out across a stranger's silk pillow case like weeds, vines, and other shit that people got rid of. I couldn't even feel my legs. Really wasn't sure I still had any after having them spread so far apart and draped over his tatted shoulders while he pounded into me like he was searching for something inside my pussy. Something I was certain he wouldn't find, and wouldn't be able to ask for if he did. Because he didn't know my name, nor did I know his.

Names seemed less than important after the third, fourth, or fifth shot. It was hard to keep count with the music being so loud and his hands being so warm against the small of my back, running the red light that was my slinky black dress, finding a spot that would render me defenseless to his touch, and applying pressure.

So much pressure.

I could still hear him breathing in my ear, breath minty, and fresh, and more intoxicating than the fireballs he'd ordered from my best friend's mobile bar at the party I was working and he was attending. I couldn't remember if he'd even drank anything. But if the throbbing between my legs was any indication, he'd either drank enough to turn into a bull, or stayed sober enough to remain the bull he already was. Either way, it was time for me to get out of his bed. Late mornings only led to niggas falling in love, and that wasn't what I'd stumbled in here for. I came to get fucked out of my mind, and he'd done that at least five times between three a.m. and whatever time it was now.

I blinked my eyes open wide enough to catch a glimpse of my shiny, black clutch sitting on a mirrored nightstand on *"my"* side of the bed. I'd heard a buzzing noise for the few minutes that I'd been awake, but it didn't occur to me that it might've been my own phone. I rolled over on my side, naked breast falling against the inside of my arm, and reached over to grab my purse and retrieve my vibrating cell.

"Nessa?" I slid the green icon and answered the call.

"Bitch, are you answering from Heaven or Hell? I've been calling you all morning!" My best and oldest friend had probably sent out an APB by now, seeing as she was the worrier of the two of us.

I sat up straight, pressing my back against the king-sized leather, tufted headboard, bringing a hand to my throbbing head. "Neither." I groaned. "Actually, it could be either. What time is it?" I didn't even have the wherewithal to look at my own damn phone screen.

"It's noon! Did you just wake up? Where the hell are you!?" Nessa fussed. I could hear her keys jingling in the background and knew right away she was gonna try to come pick me up.

Problem with that was, I had no idea where I was. And of course, I couldn't tell her that cause like I said, she was a worrier.

"I'm at a friend's." I lied. "I'll be home in an hour."

"Unless your antisocial ass has up and gotten *social* in the past twenty-four hours, *I'm* the only damn friend you have. Now tell me where you are!"

I took my eyes on a trip around the spacious bedroom that had been my chamber of lust for the last eight or so hours. Thick black drapes hung from the ceiling to the floor, pulled closed and blocking out the light so well I couldn't believe the sun was up on the other side of them. A long leather upholstered chase sat at the foot of the bed facing a tall sturdy armoire that was pushed against a far wall. Oil paintings of human silhouettes hung from all four walls, giving an almost eerie feel to the room that for some reason comforted me instead of making me feel scared. And it smelled new. Almost as if the paint on the walls had just dried. There was also a bookcase near what I'm assuming was a bedroom closet that I would've been standing in front of, taking inventory under different circumstances.

Once my eyes adjusted enough to locate my dress hanging from the corner of one of the open doors on the armoire, I scooted to the edge of the bed, moaning as I tried to stand, slowed down by the soreness between my thighs.

"Jo, what the fuck?" Nessa's voice startled me. So caught up in canvasing the room, I'd forgotten she was on the phone.

"My bad, Nessa. I was—" I paused, words interrupted by a slither of light entering the bedroom as the door crept open. The smell of bacon and maple syrup swam up into my nostrils like the sweetest gift I'd ever received without asking for it.

"Nessa, lemme call you *right* right back." I said, eyes widening as the door pushed open further.

"Oh, so you *right* rightin' me now? You shole ri—"

My thumb involuntarily pressed the end button as the phone slipped from my hand and fell back on to the mattress that was taking all my strength to leave. He stood there in the doorway, the picture of fucking perfection, wearing a pair of Houston Rockets pajama bottoms and a white T shirt that I prayed he'd let me take home, because he smelled so damned good.

He must've noticed the drunken starvation in my eyes, because he didn't even bother to ask if I was hungry. Just walked in, sat the tray in the middle of the bed, then took a seat next to me, flipped his feet up on the bed, and pulled the tray up on his lap.

A chest that chiseled and arms that ripped weren't reserved for a girl like me. I could barely handle looking at this shit, let alone fucking with it sober. And despite the fact that my stomach was turning flips, I needed to ignore the meal—hell, *both* meals—displayed before me, and climb my ass outta this man's bed before I started something I couldn't finish.

"What's wrong, you don't eat pork?" He asked, voice smooth like honey, dark brown eyes enveloping me like a warm blanket.

I could very well have been shivering from the timber in his tone touching my skin like a digit. I wanted to taste his tongue so bad—almost as bad as I wanted that bacon. Lord, I should've just jumped out the damn window when I had the chance.

"It's cool. I wouldn't wanna eat food from a stranger either." He started to put the tray back down.

But, "No!" I stopped him with a hand to his forearm. "It's just... I. What are you gonna eat?" I raised my eyes to meet his, taking in the smoothness of his chocolate, inked skin, heat pooling between my legs like it had been on the ride over in the backseat of his chauffeured SUV, when he slipped a single, thick finger into my pussy and made me cum like a fucking waterfall.

"I already ate." He pressed his back against the headboard. "I came in earlier so we could eat together but you were still passed out. Did you know you snore?" He squinted, forehead wrinkling under a perfectly lined edge-up.

"I do *not*!" I shrieked.

"Like a bear, man!" He returned with a chuckle. "It's all good, though. Snoring's cute as long as you wait til I'm asleep first."

Wait, *what*? What the hell made him think I'd be around the next time he fell asleep or the time after that? See, this is why you gotta pull the old *smash and dash*. You wake up in a nigga's bed two minutes past sunset and he's ready to make plans for all your future sleep.

"I'm sorry..." I drew a blank where his name went.

"Skoby." He filled in the blank. "And don't be sorry. Just eat this food. Cause if I throw it away, my grandma's probably gonna find out, and neither of us wants that to happen!" He grinned, sending a dimple sinking deep into one of his cheeks, just above the crisp edge of his beard. I'd vividly remembered sinking my fingers into it while his head was between my legs, and I'll be damned if I didn't shutter at the thought.

"You cold? Lemme grab you a shirt." He hopped out of the bed and retrieved a crisp white T shirt that matched the one he had on, from a chest of drawers on the opposite side of the room. I'd almost forgotten I was naked. Not that I was ever self-conscious about it. I just felt so... so covered in his presence.

And why was he being so nice? He'd literally met and fucked me the same night, yet he was treating me like we'd been dating, or at least like he wanted us to.

"I don't need it." I put a hand up as he extended the T shirt. "I gotta go." I flipped my legs off the side of the bed, feet meeting the warmest hardwood floors.

And why were his floors warm? Was it cold outside? We were well into September, but that meant nothing in Houston. It was at least eighty-five degrees out the night before.

"Sorry for the snoring." I footed over to my dress, reaching up to slide it off the hanger and dropping it over my head. "And whatever else I might've done to disturb your sleep." I continued, searching for my heels.

"No need." He stood from the bed, six-foot-something of delicious black man. "None of it was against my will." He bent over beside the nightstand, raising up with an easy smile on his face, and my shoes dangling from the tips of his fingers.

"Looking for these?" He knowingly asked, taking two slow steps toward me.

"Thank you." I took a step forward, grabbing the back straps of my shoes and looking up into his eyes when he didn't release them.

"Can we not do this?" I asked, using all the strength I had not to surrender to his scent, his face, and the undeniable churning in my pelvis in response to the fullness of his lips.

"Do what?" He looked down at me. And my eyes were

glossed with exhaustion because he had worked me the fuck out.

"Give me my shoes, Skoby, so I can go home." I kept one hand on my shoes and propped the other on my hip.

"My friends call me Bee." His grip tightened, a smirk parting his lips that had cocky written all over it.

"And I'll call you *Skoby*. Now, unass my shoes." I snapped.

"And then what?"

"And then I'll never call you anything again, because that's how these types of things work."

He shook his head, rolling his eyes up to the ceiling, probably trying to figure out what to say to get me to stay.

But he'd find nothing.

Because once I made up my mind, there was nothing anyone could do to *un-make* it.

"When can I see you again?" was what he came up with.

So much for creativity.

"I'm late for work." I quickly replied

"And you'll be later if you don't answer my question." He smiled, pretty white teeth could seduce the stripes off a tiger.

But I ain't no tiger.

"Never!" I almost yelled, frustrated by the fact that he wasn't taking the hint and I was running short on resistance. "Now gimme my damn shoes before I call the police."

"Fine." He released my shoes as I snatched them from his big hands and brushed past him in route to his open bedroom door.

Before I made it too far, having no idea where the front, back, or side door was, my stomach growled loud enough for him to hear it. I stood there, stricken with embarrassment, wishing like hell I'd grabbed the bacon off that plate. How the hell was I gonna play this off? I could've starved to death in the next five minutes.

"Take the plate." He said, brushing past me in the doorway as I wiggled my feet into my shoes. "Front door's to your left.

Driver's waiting downstairs to take you home. It was a pleasure meeting you, Joletta."

He said my name like he'd had the right, when anybody who knew me knew that the only person who'd ever called me that name had died when I was six-years-old. I ignored him, knowing he couldn't've known that, and apparently had looked in my damn purse and saw my driver's license. Then I rushed back into the room like a starving kitten, snatched that bacon off the plate along with a slice of toast, and clacked my way through the walk of shame straight down to the waiting truck.

I might not even put this shit in my journal.

"You cannot be serious right now, Jo! I stayed here all night with not one fucking word from you, now you expect me to stay all day too? You're ungrateful, you know that? You still haven't paid me from last week. This ain't no charity. And don't thank me, cause I can't pay none of my bills with that!"

You'd swear the woman lying in the bed in the room down the hallway was my birth mother and not hers, the way my aunt went on and on about how inconvenient it was to sit with her. She'd only been *"taking care"* of Mama three days a week while I went to school, worked gigs here and there with Nessa by night, and full-time at *Big Reads*—a local book store—by day. But apparently that was too much. She made a point to bitch about it as often as possible.

"I already told you they put a stop on her checks." I explained to the short round, brown-skinned woman who looked more like my birth mother than I could stomach most days. "Somebody got ahold of her debit card and a new one's on the way."

"If this is an attack on my character..." She quickly defended, grabbing her over-stuffed purse off the coffee table she was supposed to have cleared and dusted but hadn't touched.

"Nobody's attacking your anything, Aunt Janine." I snapped before I knew it, head still throbbing, in desperate need of an ibuprofen. "I'm just letting you know what's up. Why do you think I'm taking every gig? I gotta pay these bills outta my pocket or else we'll be sitting in the dark over here."

I flopped down on the sofa that had been the only sofa to grace my grandmother's living room since I was old enough to remember. She'd kept things up the best she could until health problems—mostly depression—took away her desire to do anything more than stay cooped up in her room. Then about two years back, she suffered a stroke that further limited her mobility. She could get around if she wanted to, though. I'd walked in on her preparing a full meal when she thought I'd be gone a couple of hours, and I stepped back in to grab my purse. I was convinced that the bulk of Mama's problems started the day I told her I didn't need her anymore. Putting on this needy façade was her way of keeping me close by, and I'd fallen for it hook, line, and sinker, abandoning the apartment I shared with Nessa to come back home and help her out. I'd since lost my car and pretty much my livelihood, trying to keep the both of us afloat. Mama's social security check was barely a drop in the bucket with all the bills she had waiting on the table when I showed up. And the Devil was busy at work, as usual, because as soon as I started to see some relief, somebody got ahold of Mama's debit card info and had a field day on the *Home Shopping Network*. It didn't take a rocket scientist to figure out who, since everything my Aunt Janine wore was covered in fucking rhinestones. But I couldn't afford to kick her out of our lives for being a thief. She was the only person who'd half-ass look after Mama while I was out. But you best believe her ass got frisked before she walked out the door.

In any event, Mama'd taken me in when my own mother couldn't, or wouldn't take care of me. So, sticking around to see her through whatever this was, seemed like the least I could do. I'd be lying if I said it wasn't stressful having no one else to lean on for help except her kleptomaniac daughter, who would rather be in a gambling shack, throwing away every dime she earned. Some days it seemed like I was at the bottom of a deep dark hole and would never find my way out.

"You staying or not?" I blew out a breath, hoping she'd stay, but prepared to miss out on some money if she didn't.

"Fine, lil smart ass girl." She answered, swinging her wide but shapely hips toward the door. "I need to go down to *Lucky Seven's* for a few hours first, though. Your Uncle Johnny stopped by and left me a few dollars. I need to see if I can make em grow since you got me over here working for peppermint."

A less than genuine smile crossed my dry lips as I tilted my head toward her on her way out of the door. Mama hadn't said a word since I'd walked in. But as soon as Aunt Janine left, I could hear her clearing her throat.

"Hey Mama." I pried myself off the sofa and footed down the short hallway to her room. I was surprised to find it spotless. It'd been a bit of a mess the day before. "Did Aunt Janine do this? Bout time!" I smiled at the woman who'd been the best thing to ever happen to me when I was just a little girl.

"Janine ain't did nothin but leave cigarette butts on my porch." She looked up from whatever book she was reading, dark red reading glasses sitting on the brim of her wide nose. "That's a big ole truck that dropped you off. They too good to walk you to the door?" She cut her deep-set eyes at me. Two long, gray French-braids hung over her meaty shoulders, and I was sure she'd remind me that it was time to wash and braid her hair again.

"It was a transportation service, Mama." I lied. "Lyft doesn't walk you to your door. And how'd you see all that from your bed?" I slanted my eyes at her, taking a seat in a chair that was right beside her bedroom window. The seat was still warm, which was evidence that her nosey behind had been sitting in it.

"I got my ways." She looked sideways at me over her specks, then went right back to reading.

"You been doin alotta rippin and runnin, Rene. When you gonna have time to wash my hair?" She asked without looking up,

9

the smell of mothballs filling up the small room like always.

"Tomorrow's Sunday, right?" I squinted, looking over at her with my feet folded under me in the big, red chair that used to hold my whole body with room for Mama too.

"Unless somebody changed the rules, yes, it is." She replied in her favorite language; sarcasm.

"Then tomorrow it is." I nodded, unfolding and standing from the seat to go over and kiss her forehead. "Love ya, girl." I said after planting my kiss.

"It's hard to tell." She fussed, no doubt rolling her eyes as I left the room on a tired sigh. "And when am I gonna be holding that book in my hands? I'm not gone live forever, Rene!"

I wished I'd had an answer. But the truth was I wasn't any closer to finishing my book than a cow was to jumping over the moon. My creativity hadn't been sparked in a long time. I'd barely made it through the essay I completed for *The Law of Mass Communications,* and couldn't produce more than a single paragraph for my nightly journal entries in the last few months. Mama knew that aside from her, writing was all I'd had. On most nights, if it wasn't for my journal, I wouldn't know where to put my thoughts. But I was tired. Too tired to create. In fact the only thing I had energy for was working, sleeping, and apparently, a one night stand.

Two

Skoby

The baseline to something new was blaring in my headphones, blending with the sound of my breathing while I ran the last of three miles back home through the subdivision. There wasn't much I could do with the track since I wasn't a music producer. The best I *could* do was hand it off to my boy Smitty later that night at this party he was throwing for his younger sister. The dude who was DJ'ing the party was an old friend of his, and worked full-time at a local radio station. If he thought it was worth a spin, he'd give it a spin.

And it was.

Had all the elements of a hit record, from the slow tempo on down to whoever shorty was tearing through the chorus like her next meal depended on it. The featured performer, some young cat named *Cased*, had more flow than I'd heard come through H-Town in a long time. Kinda reminded me of Z-ro but less angry. Houston would fall in love with this shit instantly.

The nerve of the dude alone was enough for me to give him a

listen. Walked up to me in the middle of a party like we were old friends and yelled his whole life story over the music in less than five minutes. Everybody knew who I was, and wouldn't dare approach me on some *come-up* shit. But this cat was the definition of desperate times calling for desperate measures. He had nothing to lose and that can send your hustle into overdrive.

To be real, the only other thing I remembered from that night was the female I'd brought home. Something about all that wild ass hair and the way she looked at me like I wasn't who I was, made me curious as fuck, and definitely put a knot in my shit. And I never did that bringing chicks home from the club shit, cause it was my experience that most females couldn't be trusted. But at the same time, I didn't feel right sending her on her way unprotected after watching her take all those shots—shots that I'd put on my tab at the bar she was working before abandoning it to turn up with me. Not that she didn't seem like she could hold her own. I just wasn't that typa nigga. And like I said, I was feeling her.

Just as I approached the driveway of the overly-sized mini-mansion my grandmother had talked me into purchasing with what she called *my first big check*, a car came screeching up beside me, the smell of weed floating in my direction as the passenger-side window went down. I didn't even have to turn around to see who it was. Where there was dro and somebody else's car, there was always Kerri. I wondered what the hell she was begging for this time.

"Bee, I know you saw me calling your damn phone!" She hopped out the passenger seat of the snow-white Nissan Sentra that was sitting on blades that probably cost half as much as the car, while her friend sat behind the wheel smearing lip gloss on her lips.

"What's the problem? Another bitch got your attention?" She propped a hand on her hip, long nails painted pink, looking me straight in the face with a set of hazel eyes that she'd passed right down to my baby girl.

Kerri was fine by all standards. Had a fat ass, slim waist, perky tits, and juicy ass lips that usually made me cum twice before I even made it to the pussy. But the down time is where she'd failed me. Conversations with her were of zero substance if we weren't discussing my daughter and her well-being. But she couldn't understand why that was a deal breaker, not even if I gave her the benefit of an explanation.

"You know I'on't keep my phone on me when I'm runnin'. What's up? Krissi aight?" I dropped my headphones around the back of my neck, grabbing a towel from the waistband of my shorts and wiping the sweat from my forehead.

Kerri couldn't see her girl behind her in the car making gestures at me with her tongue. And if she did, she'd probably invite the bitch to a threesome.

"You know what's up. Krissi's hair ain't gonna do itself." She rolled her eyes, twisting her nails through a long, silky brown weave that she'd probably paid for with a stack from the child support that was supposed to go to my daughter.

"Bet. Call Adrian. I'll shoot her the money."

"But I don't wanna go to Adrian. Her shop's in the hood. Just gimme the money and stop being a damn control freak."

This girl had known me too long to think she could pull a fast one in my baby's name. I came off too much bread every month for her to be coming at me on some extra change shit anyway, and I was only entertaining this hair-do money on the regular because my kinfolk owned a beauty salon. But now she was tripping. Tripping hard as fuck. And if she didn't figure out who she was fucking with, she was about to get embarrassed in front of her friend.

"You can miss me with that bullshit." I said, draping the towel over my shoulder and turning to walk away.

"Oh, so you don't care what yo baby look like?" She yelled from the curb. "Don't walk away from me, nigga! I didn't make her by myself and I'm not about to take care of her by myself!"

I could hear her bright pink Air Max coming up the driveway, gaining on me fast, probably preparing to smack me upside the back of my head. This was the kind of shit Kerri was used to—

fighting, and fucking, then fighting some more. But I wasn't on that. I thought I'd made it clear that the last time was the last time over a year ago, after a failed attempt to stay together for the sake of Krissi. Apparently, I didn't make myself clear.

"Sorry mother fucker!" She yelled right in my ear. I turned around fast and grabbed her arm mid-air.

"Chill." I spoke calmly. It was barely a struggle to hold her in place. She was thick, but still no match.

"I'm not chillin!" She yanked her arm. "All I'm asking for is some money to get your daughter's hair braided and you act like you ain't got it. You trickin' off on that many hoes, Bee? You takin' away from Krissi so you can impress other bitches?"

Shit was getting too loud for this time of the morning, and it was times like this when I regretted not getting those two Doberman puppies Uncle Lem told me I needed. Nothing short of a dog chasing her off my damn property would be enough.

At least that's what I thought before the front door to my crib flew open.

"Who in the hell is this out here with all that racket? The sun ain't been up a full hour yet and y'all gone have these white folks thinking we ain't got no home training!"

With Kerri's wrist still in my grasp, I looked up the driveway to find my grandmother standing in the doorway wearing a light purple house coat, and holding a piping hot plate of food.

"Gams, go back in the house! She was just about to leave!" I shouted up to her.

"It don't look like she leaving to me!" She yelled back. "Girl, have you lost your mind? Do you know how much these folks pay to keep the riff raff out? You bout to get my grandson sent back to where he came from!"

Where I *came* from was about five miles out in a nice high rise that I only moved out of to stop from catching a murder case for throwing my baby mama over the balcony. Would I have actually done it? No. Did I entertain the shit every time she came home, complaining about shit when I was giving her the world based on

14

nothing but the fact that she'd given me a child? Hell yeah.

"I'm sorry. Mrs. Paul. I'm just tryna get Krissi's hair braided and your *grandson* is giving me a hard time!" Kerri yelled past the side of my arm.

That response warranted a face-to-face conversation between her and my grandmother. "Come on in here!" She waved a hand. "This ain't the kinda thing you discuss in a damn driveway!"

"But my friend—"

"I see your friend!" Gams shouted. "Might wanna be mindful of the company you keep! Ain't nobody in their right mind gonna drive another woman around begging for money unless they need some they self! You comin in or not? This bacon and eggs ain't gonna eat itself!"

As much as she hated it—and I did too—Kerri knew there was no way around taking Gams up on that invitation. It was either carry her ass in the house to get told off in private, or have Gams come down the driveway and do it in front of her home girl. Either way, this trip was gonna be a bust. If she thought it was hard to con a dime outta me in Krissi's name, she could stack ten thousand pounds against those odds fucking with Gams.

"How long you think that girl gone sit out in the car before she drives off and leaves you?" We hadn't been seated at the breakfast bar five minutes and Gams was going in on Kerri like a stranger off the street. "And where the hell do you find somebody stupid enough to drive you somewhere you ain't wanted?"

"Mrs. Paul, I didn't—"

"You're lucky I was here." Gams cut Kerri off. I kept my focus on the plate of food in front of me, knowing I couldn't save myself or my daughter's mother once Julia Paul got ahold of her. "Driving up here with that got damn smoke coming out the windows. Your grandmother must be turning over in her grave."

15

"I'm sorry, I was just—"

"Stupid, is what you are. Kerri." Gams cut her off again. "You heard me on the intercom. Did you think I'd just sit in here while you assault Skoby in his own damn driveway? How many times have we been through this, huh? How many times you gotta come over her making a fool outta yourself before you understand that the boy don't want you?"

"Gams, look. I'mma just give her the money, aight? I gotta be somewhere in an hour and I don't have time to deal with this right now." I pushed back my barstool and stood from my seat. Kerri's eyes went wide, not knowing if Gams was gonna chill or go ape shit.

"*Fine*." Gams digressed, understanding my temperament better than anybody else. "Long as you know that if you keep giving her money, she gone keep coming back. It's like feeding a stray cat." She hopped down from her seat, swift as hell for a seventy-four-year-old woman.

"Excuse me?" Kerri squeaked. "I'm the mother of his child, and if my daughter needs something, I'm not gonna bite my tongue asking for it!"

"What your daughter *needs* is a mother that can grease her damn scalp." Gams snapped, entering the kitchen and dropping her emptied plate into a sink filled with hot, soapy dishwater. "Baby's almost five years old and you ain't learned how to comb her hair yet? I could buy a yacht with the money you spend getting Krissi's hair braided. And why ain't she been going to Adrian? Don't we get some kinda family discount?"

"I don't like—"

"Gams, chill." I cut her off. And I trembled a little inside while doing so, cause Gams was notorious for that extended back hand. "I'll cash app it." I rolled my eyes in Kerri's direction.

"I need cash." She smacked her lips.

I took a deep breath and took off down the hallway to my bedroom, grabbed a two loose hundreds from my wallet, and brought em back out to Kerri.

"Here." I laid the money on the bar top. "Tell Krissi to facetime me when her hair's finished." I lifted my chin and chunked the deuce, widening my eyes at Gams in a silent request for peace before I left her and Kerri to go take a shower.

Gams put her hands up in surrender and ushered Kerri to the door. I was surprised and relieved that the girl didn't leave with one of Gams's house slippers up her ass.

Three

Jo

It looked like a huge piece of bubble gum had exploded in these people's house. Pink balloon bouquets floating in every corner. Pink streamers hanging from the ceiling on the first floor. Pink satin ribbons wrapped around the grand staircase that split in two different directions where more pink balloons topped the railing along the banister. Even a pink runner ran from the front door and all the way up the steps, where I'm assuming the birthday girl would be making her grand entrance from under a huge arch made of three different shades of pink balloons.

Where there weren't balloons, there were pictures of her trimmed in faux pink and white diamonds. A pretty girl, brown skinned with bone straight, jet black hair styled differently in each shot to compliment several different outfits. She must've been pretty special to the host. I couldn't imagine anything this extreme for my own twenty-first birthday party. But these folks obviously had the means to throw a big ass bash, and invited my friend—or rather her mobile bartending company—to provide drinks for all the guests in attendance.

I'd been working for Nessa the night I ended up in the backseat with *Mr. Long Fingers*, and I knew she'd be giving me grief about slipping away after a gig without so much as a text message. She'd been my only constant friend since she moved into my neighborhood when we were just ten years old. She knew me almost better than I knew myself, and was always there to check me when I was losing my way. At times, Nessa felt more like a big sister than a friend. I could easily forget we were the same age if I listened to her talk without looking at her. I guess you could say somebody like me needed somebody like her and vice versa. We balanced each other out. Something like a perfectly imperfect combination.

"This kitchen is huge, right?" I tried easing in with small talk, standing behind a custom made bar in the host's kitchen between Nessa and a third bartender, Jameson.

"Huge is an understatement, girl!" Jameson flamboyantly replied, though the question was obviously directed to Nessa who hadn't said two words to me since I showed up courtesy of a talkative ass Lyft driver.

"You could bathe in that sink basin. Just look at that shit!" Jameson kept on, motioning his insanely soft hands to the long sink behind us.

"I heard they have an around the clock chef. Is he gonna be here tonight?" I asked, once again directing the question to Nessa.

"I don't know." Jameson replied. "But if this kitchen is indicative of his talent, I might need to stick around for that!" He ran a clean white drying towel around the brim of a wine glass, before placing it next to a dozen others on a serving tray he'd been prepping.

"The chef's a woman." Nessa finally spoke. "And she's already here, right on the other side of that wall. This area's strictly for the wet bar, which is why you don't see stove tops and ovens and shit. The both of you might know that if you weren't so busy being awed by every damn thing." She looked us both over then rolled her levered eyes, retrieving a black apron from the storage bin underneath the bar, and securing it around her tiny waist.

"Damn. Who pissed in your Moscato?" Jameson joked, slanting his eyes in Nessa's direction.

She didn't reply, instead placing two copies of the signature drink ingredients on the bar-top for us to look over. *Bubble Gum Martinis* were the birthday girl's signature drink for the night. A typical sweet choice for someone being introduced to alcohol for the first time.

I tried not to sweat Nessa's attitude because I knew how she got when she had shit on her chest. But if we were gonna be tending bar together, we'd be in close quarters all night, and it'd be nearly impossible to avoid the huge elephant in the room. Jameson had worked with us enough times to pick up on the static, and luckily, he knew when to pull back too, or get cursed the fuck out in these people's house.

After serving what had to be at least five dozen *Bubble Gum Martinis* to a crowd green enough to still have a curfew, we'd made it midway through the event. The music selection was questionable. Note after annoying note of mumble rap and other shit that could very well have been in another damn language. I was tired as hell, having had less than five hours of sleep before showing up. And the fact that Nessa still hadn't said a word to me was making things even worse.

Then suddenly, from the corner of my eye, I spotted a reason to make her speak. My heart felt like it might beat out of my chest, and I wished I could melt into the damn floor.

"Nessa, I need to run to the restroom!" I leaned to the side and yelled at her over the music.

"What? It can't wait? Did you see the gang of niggas that just walked in?" She looked at me like I was crazy.

"I did, and that's why I need to slip away right quick!" I said, taking my eyes back to the patio door where I'd seen him walk in. "Please. I'll explain later. Just—"

"Excuse me, y'all busy?" That smooth as honey voice came from the very area I hadn't canvased. He was right in front of my face. It was too late to run, and Nessa was looking straight at me.

"We're not!" She rolled her eyes from me to him. "What can I get you?" She asked with a smile, bracing her manicured palms on top of the bar.

"And if she can't get it, I'm sure I can!" Jameson offered flirtatiously. He didn't typically hit on men without knowing if they were batting for the same team first, but Skoby was the type that gave you no choice but to shoot your shot.

"I'm good on all that, bruh." Skoby looked Jameson straight in the face. And if looks could kill, my boy woulda been on his way to the coroner's office.

"Actually, I was hoping maybe Joletta could help me." He softened his death stare on Jameson and brought those woodsy browns to me, letting my name swim off the brim of his juicy lips, pissing me off and turning me on at the same time.

I took a deep breath and cleared my throat, then asked, "What'll you have?"

He replied with a smirk, "You know what I like."

Nessa and Jameson almost lost their shit, watching me with their eyes about to fall outta their damn heads, as I stood their pretending my fucking panties weren't soaked.

"Water." He said, grinning and amused by my friends' reaction to his drink order.

"Tap or bottled?" I reached under the counter to grab a clean drinking glass and filled it with ice.

"Bottled, please." His request was soft and sincere. Nothing like the savage beast that had ripped off my *good* panties and fingered me to oblivion.

"Dasani okay?" I asked, secretly craving the sound of his voice in any capacity.

"*Preferred.*" He nodded, reaching back and pulling a wallet from the pocket of a pair of deep gray slacks that were a risky match to the pink button down that was hugging his chest like I wanted to.

I grabbed a bottle of water from beside the drinking glasses and poured it over the ice while his eyes stayed glued to me. The ice shifted as the water almost reached the top of the glass. I looked up from it, taking inventory of his resting Adam's apple and neatly manicured beard, remembering how good those lips felt suckling hard at my nipples.

"You gonna give the man his drink or not, Jo?" Nessa spoke up, snapping me out of the hypnosis that this man had put me in.

"Sorry. Here you go." I laid out a napkin in front of him and placed the cool drink on it.

"S'all good. 'Preciate it." He laid a crisp one-hundred dollar bill beside the glass, picked up his drink, then winked at me before turning to walk away.

"Umm, bitch you better grab that before I do!" Jameson eyed the bill like the money hungry fiend he was. "I got bills due, and if you don't want it—"

"I can't accept that." I cut him off. "Nessa, I can't accept that right? Water's complimentary."

"It's a tip, *Honest Abe*!" She elbowed me in the side. "Take it, or I will."

I snatched the money off the bar-top and untied the apron from around my waist. "I'll be right back." I nodded to Nessa.

"Girl, where are you going? We got two more hours before this thing ends!" She said as I slid past her from behind the bar.

"I'm taking this money back. You know ain't nothin free. This nigga thinks he can buy me like some cheap hoe off the street, and that ain't so. I'll be back, I promise."

I rushed off, searching for the arrogant son-of-a-bitch who apparently thought I'd be impressed by him dropping one hundred fucking dollars for a twelve ounce glass of ice-water. It didn't take long to locate him. Seemed like he was waiting for me to come running.

"Excuse me, what the hell is this?" I approached him just outside the luxurious estate, leaning against the railing of a raised patio adjacent to the front door.

"It's a tip. This your first one?" He cracked a smile and I'll be damned if I didn't wanna slap it off his handsome fucking face.

"Don't play with me, Skoby. Here!" I extended the money in his direction.

"So, you remembered my name?" He tipped his chin up, still leaning against the railing, long arms folded across his chest.

"Will you just take the money? I need to get back inside." I huffed.

"And so do I." He stood and walked toward me. "Come chill with me tonight." He suggested, so close to me now, that I could smell that damn cologne.

"I thought I made it clear, that was a one and done situation." I took a step back, arm still extended with his money in my hand. "Take this, please."

"I'm not takin that." He pushed my hand away. "That's not what I want." He stepped in even closer. "And that's not what you want either, if we're being honest."

"*We* ain't being shit!" I shoved the money into his chest. And my God, why'd I do that? Touching him did nothing but intensify the pull.

"Listen, you're a nice dude. Probably the best looking one in this whole damn party, and I'm not the only one to notice that. You could go in there and have your pick from all those aunties."

"You know what, you right." He nodded. "But I'm still not taking that tip back."

"Uncle Bee, come on! We're about to cut the cake!" The young lady, Brittani, from all the pictures came busting through the door. "She's cute! *Hey, Auntie!*" She jotted her eyes from Skoby to me, smiling so hard it was almost contagious.

"Hi, I'm not his—"

"It's okay." She cut me off. "Uncle Bee's always tryna keep me outta his business. But I'll find out. I have my ways!" She grabbed his hand and took off into the house, looking back over her shoulder and waving for me to join them, with a waist length ponytail swinging from the crown of her head.

Skoby didn't object, knowing damn well there was nothing to find out about.

We fucked.

It was good.

The end.

I trailed on in behind them, still holding the money I hadn't earned, dead-set on putting it back in his stubborn ass hands.

"So, you just left? Knowing I didn't have a damn ride, you just left me out here at a fucking stranger's house? So much for friendship, Vanessa!"

It was breezy as shit, and quiet outside on the steps of this house that was way too big for my liking. Most of the party goers had left, and I was the last of *Nessa's Mobile Bar* staff to leave the event. I'd stayed behind to clean up things as a kiss-up favor for bailing on her at the last gig. But when she told me she was going home, I didn't take her seriously. I didn't think the bitch would actually leave me stranded. Like what part of the friendship game was this?

"Bitch, it's the Woodlands. You safe!" She chuckled. "Besides, this won't be your first time staying over a stranger's house this week." She laughed into the receiver, wind blowing as she drove down the road with her windows down.

"You can go straight to hell!" I hissed into the phone, stepping to the side as one of the guests accidentally brushed my arm on the way out of the door.

"Did he take it back?" She asked on the end of a chuckle.

"No." I replied dryly.

"Good. Cause he's fine as fuck and it'd be a shame for a man that fine to be an Indian giver."

"Yeah, I noticed." I sighed.

"So, what's the problem?"

"What problem?" I squeaked, now making my way to the bottom of the steps toward the u-shaped driveway where a few folks were waiting for the valet to bring up their cars.

"Don't play with me, Jo. Just the other night, this nigga had you so occupied that you couldn't even answer your phone. Now you're playing hard to get? Girl, bye!"

Clacking down the gravel walkway in four-inch heels, wearing a skirt that showed damn near the entire length of my legs, I adjusted my bag on my shoulder and put Nessa on speakerphone while I opened the Lyft app.

"I don't know when it became so difficult to comprehend the meaning of a one-night stand, but I can give a refresher course if you need one." I chuckled, shaking my head and waiting for the closest Lyft to pop up.

"Whatever." Nessa laughed. "Just make sure you have two slots available, cause obviously, I'm not the only one who needs a refresher. That brother couldn't take his eyes off your lil angry ass."

"He was thirsty." I smacked my lips, still waiting on this slow ass app to load.

"Yeah, and not for that one hundred dollar ass water!" Nessa was really with the shits tonight.

"Vanessa, you can stop."

"And you can *go!*" She snapped. "And fast before somebody with more sense picks up what your ass is dropping. That man smelled like money, Jo. And if that bulge in his slacks is an honest one, cash ain't the only thing he's packing!"

I think Nessa forgot that she was driving and clapped her damn hands while cackling into the phone.

"If I didn't love you like a distant relative, I'd be insulted." I said. "I don't need his money or his *dick* for that matter."

"Oooh, but you do!" She said. "At least the dick part. You be way too tensed up most days, sis. Let that man blow your back out a few more times before you drop him. It won't kill you."

A deep sigh flowed from my mouth after five minutes of not being able to get my Lyft app to open. I took Nessa off the speaker and put the phone up to my ear. "Look, I'm gonna have to call you back." I said. "This phone's tripping and I need to request a Lyft."

"Cool. Hit me up when you make it home… or wherever!"

"Home is where I'll be. Bye, bitch!"

I ended the call and went right back to the app. Still no luck and almost all the damn guests were gone. Aside from shaking hands and taking drink orders, I didn't know these people well enough to be asking to use their phones. Frustration must've been written all over my face when the only person I *kinda* knew walked up beside me and offered to assist.

"You good?" Honey. Smooth as fucking honey.

"Seriously? Are you stalking me?" I turned to face him, looking straight up into his eyes and trying hard not to breathe him in.

"Don't answer that." I put a hand up, and looked back down at my phone.

"I wasn't planning on it." He replied. "Reception's trash out here. I could give you a ride if you can't get that app up."

"*Or*, you could let me use your phone to order a Lyft." I reached to my side and dropped my phone in my bag, then looked back up at the man I couldn't seem to shake.

"Nah. I'on't know you like that." A handsomely flirtatious smile spread across his bearded face, rendering me damn near defenseless all over again. And I hadn't had a drop to drink.

"Yet you're willing to let me in your car?" I piped.

"Well, I already had you in my bed. It's hardly a task."

"Excuse—"

"Hold up! I ain't mean it like that." He cut me off with a hand to my waist. I lowered my eyes to the veins running under his deep chocolate skin, and had to bite my lip to stop from raising up on my tiptoes and shoving my damn tongue down his throat.

"Just lemme give you a ride. I ain't asking for nothin. Just tryna look out."

"Fine." I exhaled. "As long as you know I don't need you for this or nothin else. My friend's just… she left me in a shitty situation. That's it and that's all."

"You ain't gotta explain nothing to me, Lil Mama." He reached out a hand as his driver pulled up. "You want me to grab that or…"

"I got it. Thanks." I tipped my head to the side, stepping forward as he made his way to the back seat of the SUV and motioned for me to climb in first while he held the door open, shaking his head and getting an eye full of my ass.

Skoby

I liked it quiet, but not this quiet. Seemed like she was more fixated on her phone than she was on me, and that woulda been fine if I could've done the same thing. But I couldn't. Was seriously fighting the urge to go over and sit next to her and get a whiff of that vanilla scent she'd left on my pillow case, and maybe even rub a hand down between those chocolate thighs. Jo was bad. Wasn't even in the same category with most of the females I came in contact with. Pretty faces and fat asses came a dime a dozen in my circle, but they never pulled at my curiosity the way this woman did. I don't know, maybe it was just the thrill of the chase. I hadn't played that game since high school.

"See somethin you like over here?" She peeped up at me out of the corner of her eye, still swiping away at that damn phone with less than two feet of space between us as I sat directly across from her.

I shook my head without speaking. I had a feeling she got more satisfaction from looks than words, and I was doing all I could to play it cool. After a brief moment of nothing but the Isley Brothers playing through the speakers—courtesy of Uncle Lem— she dropped her phone in an oversized bag that was housing God knows what. I'd been checking a few notifications on my own phone since I hadn't looked at it for the duration of the party. Then a slight movement from across the way caught one hundred percent of my attention.

One of those toned, chocolate legs was crossed over the other. The skinny heel of one of her shoes dug into the just-cleaned carpeting on my floor board, while the other dangled next to her calf, pulling my eyes to an almost fully exposed thigh. She was staring at me, midnight eyes contradicting all the shit she was talking, about not wanting or needing me. She might not've wanted that outrageous tip I left her, but it was clear she wanted something else. Flashing a flirtatious smile that made my groin tighten, she slowly uncrossed her leg. Running her hands over her thighs, her stare grew more intense, to the point that I actually felt myself getting hot. I was being hypnotized. Every part of me was under her control. Slacks started feeling tighter at the crotch, and I couldn't stop this shit if I wanted to.

On the surface, I probably looked calm and collected, but my heart rate was a direct contradiction as she slipped both hands down between her thighs and pushed her legs apart, sending that short skirt rolling up to the top of her hips. It was too dark to tell from that angle, but I could've sworn she wasn't wearing panties. And just as if she'd read my mind, she pulled one hand from between her legs, and clicked on the overhead light.

That chocolate pussy with the pretty pink center that I'd been craving since the last time I tasted it, was now fully exposed under a spot light, sending my dick into a painful swell. With her eyes still on me, watching me grip my dick, she slid her fingers down her slick folds, wet noises from between her legs damn near drowning out the music. So many questions ran through my mind:

Is she gonna let me taste it?

Will it be as sweet as the first time?

Will she let me put the tip in?

Maybe a little bit more than the tip?

Was she walking around the party that whole time with no fucking panties on!?

Ok, that last one kinda fucked with me. My boys had been checking her out almost as hard as me. And if she'd so much as bent over to pick up a napkin they would've seen everything. The thought of that, of them seeing her most intimate parts, pissed me off for reasons that I couldn't make sense of.

So, I asked, with my dick throbbing in my fucking pants, "Where yo panties at?"

"In my purse." She purred, pretty eyes blinking shut as she slipped a finger inside her pussy.

"Why?" My voice cracked like I was going though puberty, trying not to jack off when it was all I wanted to do.

Grinding against her palm, she moaned, "Cause they were wet!" She slid a finger out of her pussy, shoved it in her mouth and licked it clean, then spread her legs open wider and started fingering herself again.

I felt the truck slowing, and yelled "Keep driving, Unc!" since we'd probably reached Jo's place, and I didn't need Uncle Lem walking around to open the door with Jo's entire pussy on display.

The truck accelerated over a bump in the road, sending Jo's titties bouncing under a jet black, low cut, spandex top. It took everything in me not to leave my seat, massaging my dick through my pants while she wildly fingered her pussy. Her legs were open so wide that I could see straight up her slit. Her pussy was creaming wet, and her head full of jet black coils fell back against the headrest as she force fed fingers to her slick pussy lips. She was about to make me watch her cum, to which I had no objection. Jo was panting, lips parting to catch her breath, as she struggled to keep her eyes open through the threat of an orgasm.

Letting down my guard a little, I spread my legs apart and

fisted my dick through my pants while watching her play, trying my best to keep up with the shit she was doing across from me without reaching over and pulling her onto my lap.

"Aaahhh!" She moaned. That soft ass voice sent my dick to rock solidness. She rubbed two fingers up and down her swollen clit, still rocking hard against the fingers that were inside her pussy. I squeezed my dick harder while she stared at me with lust and desperation painted on her face, urging her to cum so I could follow suit, and maybe get a replay of what we'd done the night before.

"Fuck!" She bit down on her bottom lip, hips rolling, naked ass sliding back and forth against my leather seats as she grinded out a nut on her own fingers. She threw her head back, eyes rolling to the back of her head, making a mess on my seat, squirting like a fucking fire hydrant while I kept on pulling my shit.

This shit is stupid.

Why can't I stop?

She ain't even touching me, and I'm bout to pop.

Heat coursed through my groin, nuts tingling beneath a hard dick, ready to be emptied at any moment. Jo spread her legs wider, leaning farther back against the seat, titties jumping as she grinded against her fingers, sliding them up and down her slit. I wanted to lick her pussy so bad I could taste it on my tongue. I was pulling my shit so hard, waiting to cum almost hurt. She slapped her pussy hard, sucking her teeth from the pain it must've caused, staring at me while she did it, titties rising and falling as she moaned and breathed deep, nipples beading beneath the thin fabric of her top. It wasn't long before my eyes had seen enough. Her legs were so wide open that she might as well have been doing the splits. I squeezed down the length of my dick until my thumb grazed the head. And with my legs shivering, eyes fixed on this beautifully nasty mother fucker across from me, climax swam to the head of my dick, and I exploded, making a mess in my fucking boxers.

Jo

Not a word was spoken as he reached into a hidden compartment beneath his seat, glaring at me like I'd committed a crime, with cum staining the inside of his slacks. I couldn't see it on the outside of his pants, but I'd seen his *cum face* enough times that one night, to know that that's exactly what had happened. He unbuttoned his pants and quickly wiped himself clean, then retrieved another towel from the same compartment, sliding forward in his seat, eyes still on me like a hawk. I thought I'd gotten all my rocks off, but apparently, there was at least a little left as Skoby reached across the small space between us, gently parted my knees, and wiped clean the mess that I'd made on myself and his smooth, leather seat, sending chills up my fucking spine. As hard as it was to admit it at this point, I really wanted to hear his voice, even if it was just to say *fuck you!* But the silence was all my fault after playing this game in the first place. The man probably thought I was crazy. And for the most part, he was absolutely right.

Like some evil trick from the universe, the intro of *Voyage to Atlantis* played over the crisp sound system, instantly reminding me of the last time I'd seen my Daddy alive. I'd avoided those types of memories on a daily basis, certain that if I didn't, I'd start crying and never stop. For the life of me I couldn't understand why of all songs, that one would come on while I was in the most compromising positon. But then again, my pops did have a sense of humor. Maybe he was sending his baby girl a sign to sit her fast ass down somewhere.

"Can you turn that down?" I asked, swallowing a lump in my throat that'd surfaced from out of nowhere.

"Why, you wanna talk now?" He grinned, dropping both soiled towels in a corner close to his door, fastening his pants and resting his forearms on his thighs.

"No. I just don't wanna hear that song." I shook off an emotional sniffle, straightening my skirt, eyes down on my shoes.

"You good?" Skoby asked with concern in his voice, reaching up and pressing a button next to the sunroof, and a panel covered in buttons dropped down; one of which he used to turn the music down.

"I'm fine." I lied.

I didn't have time to pour out my life story to somebody who probably had more important things to do, but was too hypnotized by my pussy to remember them at the moment. And aside from that, I needed to get home to Mama before Aunt Janine started blowing up my phone.

"I can walk from here." I spoke before he had a chance to question me again. The look on his face said he didn't believe me when I told him I was ok, and I didn't feel like going back and forth about it.

He breathed in, sliding back against his seat and said, "Stay with me tonight."

"That's not gonna happen." I replied dryly, glad to switch my thoughts but still not willing to take him up on the offer.

"Why not?" He asked.

"Cause I don't want to." I returned, eyes scrunched.

"Then what the fuck was that?" He spread his hands out over his lap, palms facing up.

"It was me pleasing myself, and you were lucky enough to watch."

"You couldna waited til you got home to do to do that shit?" He asked, smirking and noticeably irritated.

"Of course I could've. But what fun would that be!?" I winked.

Skoby didn't say a word. Just shook his head and took a deep breath in. I'll be the first to admit that giving this man a peep show without giving him the actual pussy was borderline childish. But in my defense, I was equally as riled up watching him massage his dick. There really were no winners in this game.

Part of me didn't wanna leave any more than he wanted to let me. But I needed to. Almost every bad decision I'd ever made started with a feeling instead of common sense. And in that moment, while my feelings were telling me to go home with Skoby and ride him to sleep, common sense was telling me that he wasn't what I needed. Hell, he didn't even know who I was.

"That's childish as fuck." He hissed out a chuckle. "Unc, pull over!" He tapped on the partition that separated us from the front of the truck.

The vehicle came to a rolling stop along the curb a few feet up the block from my house. I slipped my bag up on my shoulder and slid toward the door, feeling Skoby's eyes on me the entire time, dropping the one hundred dollar bill that I'd balled up in my hand on his floor board and sliding it under the seat.

"Lemme get that." He reached across me, his cool crisp scent exciting my senses, and pulled the door handle, pushing the door open and stepping out to hold it open for me. "I'll walk your childish ass to your door." He smirked, extending a strong hand to help me out of the truck. I gripped it until both my heels touched the pavement then quickly pulled it away.

"I'm fine. Thanks." I said, stepping up onto the sidewalk.

"Joletta—"

"Don't call me that!" I snapped.

"My bad." He put a hand to his chest. "*Jo,* y'all barely got street lights. I'm just tryna make sure you get home safe."

"And who said that's your responsibility?" I asked, emotions as wild and all over the place as my hair, as he stood there frustrated shoving his hands in his pockets.

"The folks who raised me, that's who. Now stop trippin and walk." He pulled his hands from his pockets and pressed at the small of my back, and I'd be lying if I said I wasn't turned on by the authority in his tone. Nobody told me what to do, and the fact that he thought he could made my pussy wet all over again.

"Fine!" I rolled my eyes up at him, adjusted my purse strap and took off walking, panty-less ass bouncing behind me with his eyes glued to it, I'm sure.

As we neared the house, I noticed that my Aunt Janine's car wasn't parked outside.

"I know this bitch didn't leave." I fumed under my breath. *"Fuckin triflin'."* I quickened my steps.

"What?" Skoby had overheard me and stopped his stride.

"Oh, it's… I wasn't talking to you." I turned around to apologize. "And this is my stop. So...thanks. You can go now." I looked up into his eyes then quickly turned back around to sift through my purse for keys.

"Aight." I heard his shoes crackling against the sidewalk as he took a step back and slid his hands back in his pockets. "Take care, man." He said before I peeped up from my purse to watch him walk away. Mother fucker had the nerve to be bowlegged.

"Rene, is that you?" I heard Mama yelling from the other side of the door, pulling my eyes from the slightly bowlegged man I'd just sent away.

She pulled the door open before I could get my keys together, then peeped her head out and asked, "Who is that?" just loud enough for Skoby to hear her.

"It's nobody, Mama. What're you doin outta bed?" I tried

pushing my way in while she squinted her deep brown eyes tryna get a better look at Skoby.

And I couldn't blame her. The man was top shelf wine fine, striding down the sidewalk like he owned the damn block.

"He don't look like *nobody* to me. Hey, anybody told you it's rude not to introduce yo' self when you come to somebody's house!?" She leaned on her walker and yelled right past me in Skoby's direction.

"Mama, *please!*"

I begged her to step back into the house as Skoby turned around with a hand to his chest, mouthing *"Me?"*

"Yeah *you!*" Mama yelled again. "You the only one hurrying off down the street like you done stole somethin'!"

"Mama, just leave the man alone." I pressed a hand to her shoulder. "Let's get you back inside, okay?" I reached in to push the door open, on edge as she carefully backed into the house.

"I don't understand why you keep going for these good-for-nothin' negroes." She fussed, big behind bumping the side table at the entry to our small home, somehow managing to knock all gazillion whatnots sitting on top of it onto the floor.

"Oh, Lord. Look what I done did!" Mama, gripped the handles on her walker, face scrunched with disappointment.

"It's ok, Mama. I got it." I said, stooping down to pick up all the wooden figurines that had been sitting on that table longer than I'd been alive.

"Need some help?" Deep, honey drenched chords sounded from the open door, the crisp invigorating smell of his cologne riding on the cool breeze that followed him. Mama's walker clacked against the hardwood floors as she braced herself, looking up at Skoby like she'd just seen The Lord himself.

"Sorry ma'am, I'm Skoby." He nodded in Mama's direction.

"Woulda told you that before I left, but your daughter sent me off."

He slanted those eyes down at me, trimmed beard glistening in the dim light of our living room. He was a sight for sore eyes, no doubt. But I wasn't about to play this game.

"Hmmph." Mama's chest puffed, dragging her eyes from Skoby to me. "And why would you do that, Rene? Send a perfectly good-lookin' man away when you know I ain't had one in decades!?"

"Mama!?" I screeched.

"What? Don't nothin' get old but clothes!" She chuckled, and for some disgusting reason, Skoby thought that was funny too.

"You know what, stop it!" I put a hand up and got up from the floor. "He gave me a ride."

"I bet he did…" Mama curved her lips and rolled her eyes, winking at Skoby as she made her way to the worn sofa and backed up close to it.

"You need some help, Miss?" He asked, hesitantly stepping halfway through the door.

"It's Mama Jo. And yes." Mama replied.

Fast ass.

"It's fine. I got her." I stepped away from the mess I was cleaning up, almost colliding with him as he entered the living room.

"No, you worry about getting my *wood folk* up off the floor." Mama winked at Skoby, and he ate that shit up, glancing over his broad shoulder to taunt me. "I think Mr. Skoby's more qualified for this over here!" She added as he grabbed one of her hands before sliding her walker out of the way with his foot like a seasoned CNA.

Before I knew it, he'd placed her hands on his shoulders, and had his hands planted at either side of her waist, lowering her onto the sofa without losing a single breath. I didn't know how to feel about it, having him in my house, handling the person who meant the most to me like an old, familiar friend. But the smile on Mama's face was one I hadn't seen in a while, and I was a little salty that I hadn't put it there.

"You know, you sure do look familiar." She said, scooting back on the couch as Skoby stood from helping her down. "Who's ya people?" She asked.

"Ah, you probably don't know 'em." Skoby grinned, stepping away from Mama and putting those hands back in his pockets.

"Try me." She said.

And I hated when she did that. Mama would literally have a person spitting out names for half an hour tryna figure out where she knew them from.

"Well, I was raised by my grandparents, Avis and Julia Paul."

Mama curled her lips and squinted up at Skoby. "Nah, can't say I know any Pauls." Her voice squeaked. "I'll figure it out before you leave here. I'd never forget a face like that."

At this point, Skoby was full on blushing, sharp jawline pulled into a handsome smile that made my nipples hard. I was certain he was about to tell Mama he had to go since his uncle had been sitting outside waiting with the truck running. So imagine my surprise when he took her up on an offer to stay and have a bowl of chicken and dumplings.

Not a good journal entry at all.

Skoby

She said she hadn't cooked in over three years, but you wouldn't know that from the taste of her chicken and dumplings. I don't know if it was her intention, but Mama Jo had managed to make me feel like family in less than two hours. She was a lot more hospitable than her mean ass granddaughter, whom she claimed was as sweet as pie under that tough exterior.

After dinner and a slice of homemade German Chocolate cake that made me wish I'd brought Tupperware, Jo went off to the back of the house to get Mama Jo's room squared away before bed, leaving us alone in the living room to chop it up a little more. She'd run down a list of damn near two dozen people, tryna figure out where she knew me from. Then finally, a bell was struck that would blow my mind as well as hers.

"You know what, I think I done figured it out." A set of dark, catlike eyes that looked just like Jo's lit up like lightbulbs. "Did your grandfather own a fruit truck?" She asked.

"Yes ma'am. Well, kinda." I replied, sitting up and resting my forearms on my knees. "He owned a produce company. State wide distribution center, actually. *Paul's Freshest.*"

"Then that explains where I know that face! *Fruit Man* used to come through this neighborhood every Thursday afternoon like clock-work. I might have a picture of him somewhere around here if you got a minute."

I honestly didn't have a minute. It was late as hell and Uncle Lem had been circling the neighborhood waiting for me to come out for the past two hours. I'd offered for him to come in and sit, but he'd declined for whatever reason. But I couldn't get up and leave without seeing if Mama Jo actually had a picture of Gramps.

"Yeah, I um. Yes ma'am. I'd like to see that picture if it's not too much." The words almost got lodged in my throat. Just the thought of somebody outside of immediate family knowing Gramps and having any type of story to share made my heart race. I'd missed him more than I cared to talk about, cause he'd been gone so long that it seemed like I should've been over it. He'd been the only man to invest in me without asking for anything in return. He's the reason I tried so hard to stay on the right path.

"Alright, gimme a minute." She tried pushing up from the sofa.

"Is it somewhere close by? You don't have to get up." I stood from the couch ready to help.

"Yeah, it's right up under that coffee table." She pointed to a worn coffee table in the center of the room that looked like it had seen better days, but with a little attention, could see a few more.

"That red photo album is where I put the picture, I believe." She wagged her plump finger, and I went over to retrieve the old worn out photo album from the bottom of a stack of books that were in the same condition.

Easing back down on the couch beside her, I watched like a kid on Christmas Day as she slowly flipped through the pages, most of them pictures of a smiling little girl with big hair, who had to be Jo. An older man was present in a few of em, and two other ladies that could pass for twins, who looked less like Mama Jo and more like the older man. None of the pictures in this album were recent. Made me wonder where those other folks went.

Toward the last few pages, I started to lose hope, even looked up a few times to see what was taking Jo so long to come out of that back room. Then a holler left Mama Jo's mouth that made me straighten my back. I looked down at her smooth, brown hands to see a picture of Gramps as clear as day, passing fresh fruit to people I didn't know from the back of his old red fruit truck.

"When was this picture taken, Mama Jo?" My throat tightened. I had never seen my grandfather in this light.

He was a charitable man, always writing checks for this or making donations for that. But I'd never seen him so hands-on. It was like I was looking at a stranger.

"Oh, this had to be around two thousand two." She ran her thumb over his picture, staring at it the way that people stare at things when they're reminiscing. "This was the last time we ever saw *Fruit Man*. Never heard nothin' else from him."

I sat there quiet, knowing that the reason she never heard from him again was because he died that year on my eighteenth birthday. I'd had plenty of shitty days in my life, but the day I lost the only father I ever knew—on my birthday, no less—had to be one of the worst.

"I take it from the look on your face *Fruit Man* ain't with us no more?" Mama Jo placed a gentle hand on top of mine, rubbing the back of my palm as if she knew that was what I'd needed.

"He was a good man." She said. "One of the best. Might sound crazy but these kids were happier to see that red fruit truck coming than they were to see the ice cream man!" Her meaty shoulders went up in a laugh that came from her gut. I had to shake my head and swallow the tingling in my throat. I couldn't be at this woman's house crying and shit.

"You mind if I take this picture with me?" I asked, staring at the picture as if it might bring him back to life. "I just wanna get a copy made and I'll bring it right back."

"Go 'head." She nodded, pushing a thumb under the plastic sleeve that held the picture. "Don't be too long about it, now. I think this might be the only picture we got of *Fruit Man*. He was funny about taking pictures. Rene snapped this one when he wasn't looking."

I couldn't take my eyes off of it. He was wearing his favorite red shirt that had his company name, *Paul's Freshest*, written in bold white lettering across the top. The smile on his face was the same one I remembered seeing that morning before he died, when he handed me a T shirt just like his and told me that shirt held the key to every birthday gift I'd ever give myself or anybody else for the rest of my life. I'd gone over his last words to me so many times that it damn near drove me insane. Couldn't help thinking that there was something I could've done. He was damn near telling me good bye that day and I couldn't even see it. I'd been with him and Grams since I was six. Knew the man better than I knew the back of my hand. But on the day that would ultimately be his last on earth, I didn't realize that he was preparing me to live without him. What the hell could've been blocking my view?

"Here." I reached in my pocket and pulled out the hundred dollar bill that Jo didn't think I saw her slide under the seat in my truck.

"What's this?" Mama Jo's face did something between a frown and a smile. "I hope you ain't tryna buy a good time. Baby, I ain't rode nothin but my wheelchair in at least two decades!"

"Nah. *No*! No ma'am !" I busted out laughing. Mama Jo was a piece of work. "It's for the picture. Actually, just the memory. I appreciate you sharing it with me." I squeezed her hand, transferring the money from my palm to hers.

"Oh, ok." She nodded, smiling as she hesitantly accepted the gift.

"And if you don't mind, can we keep this between us? I don't like putting my business out there like that." I asked, tilting my head toward the hallway that Jo had gone down, hoping she'd get my drift.

"If you're asking me to keep this from Rene, you got it." She slanted her stare to the hallway. "That girl would rather work a year straight with no days off than to take a dime from a stranger. I, on the other hand, ain't got no problem accepting gifts. 'Specially not from the *Fruit Man's* handsome grandson!" She winked and pinched my cheek. Her hands smelled just like cocoa butter.

"Alright, Mama. Your bed's ready." Jo appeared from down the hall wearing a light gray mid-drift sweater and navy yoga pants that hugged her curves like a second skin.

I stood to help Mama Jo up off the couch, whispering thanks for her keeping this secret, hit by a sweet vanilla scent as Jo brushed past me to grab the walker. Had she been back there taking a shower the whole time? She was taking this tease shit to a whole 'nother level.

42

"Thank you, baby." Mama Jo nodded, letting go of my hand and bracing both her palms on the bar of her walker.

I stepped aside and let Jo take over, placing her hands at the small of her grandmother's back and walking alongside her out of the living room. "Don't be a stranger, Skoby!" Mama Jo yelled over her shoulder. "And don't you pay my granddaughter no mind. She ain't nothin' but cotton candy underneath all that concrete!"

Jo shook her head and rolled her eyes at me before disappearing down the hallway beside Mama Jo. After settling her into bed, she came back out to the living room, looking beautiful and exhausted. Shit was really getting to me.

"Thank you." I spoke before she did, certain that she'd ruin this made for TV moment with a smart-ass remark.

"For what?" She asked, hand propped on her hip. "I didn't invite you in here tonight, and I won't be inviting you in the future. My grandma's lonely. You could've been a stray dog and she would've let you in and fed you that same damn chicken and dumplings out of that same damn bowl. But I'm not her, so don't think that—what are you doing?"

She stopped talking, noticing that I'd started taking steps toward her. "I'm listening." I said.

"No, you're approaching me when you should be approaching the door." She pointed a finger toward a heavy wooden door that could use a few coats of fresh paint.

"I'm a grown man, Jo. I know how to navigate a living room." I kept on stepping until I was right in front of her face, looking down into her eyes, inhaling her soft scent, and watching her pretend she didn't wanna taste my tongue as much as I wanted to taste hers.

She folded her arms across her chest, wild hair pulled back into a ponytail, all traces of make-up cleaned from her face. I wanted to wrap this girl up in my arms so bad it didn't make sense. Wished I could sweep her off her feet and take her back to my crib.

But she wasn't having that. I'd damn near begged and wound up with nothing but cum in my boxers. Even with that being the case, I couldn't resist touching her before I walked out the door. So I leaned in before she could see it coming, and placed a kiss on her forehead just like the man in all those pictures had done.

"Have a good night." I said, the sweetness of her skin lingering on my lips.

She didn't say a word, just watched me walk away, staring at me as I looked over my shoulder before pulling the door closed.

Four

Skoby

"That's your grandpa, alright!" Gams held the picture I'd gotten from Mama Jo up to her face, smiling like a Cheshire cat. "I wouldn't be surprised if this man was running a circus on Wednesdays behind my back. He was always up to something!"

"Wait, so you didn't know about this either?" I asked, flopping down on the sofa across the room from her. She'd just gotten back in town from a cruise I sent her and a friend on. Gams was spoiled rotten. Could literally ask me for anything and I'd break my neck to make sure she got it.

"Oh, baby, there are so many things I didn't know about your grandfather." She tucked her feet under her and pulled a plush pillow from behind her back, resting her elbow on the arm of the couch.

"If I had a dollar for every time somebody stopped me in the grocery store telling me about how he'd paid for their groceries or bought Christmas gifts for their children, I'd be a millionaire by now." She chuckled, eyes still fixed on a picture of the only man she'd ever loved.

"Man." I leaned back against the cushions, laid a hand behind my head, and kicked my feet up on the leather ottoman in front of my sofa. "Mama Jo said he came around every Thursday. Why Thursdays?" I asked, having no recollection of that day being special for any reason.

"It'd probably be better to ask your Uncle Lem about that." Gams replied, looking up from the picture and taking a deep breath.

"You aight?" I sat up, taking notice of her changed demeanor. "Gramps wasn't steppin' out on you, was he?" I had to ask. Me and Gams kept it one hundred at all times. I knew she wouldn't trip about me asking.

"Boy, no!" She laughed. "I was the undisputed apple of your grandpa's eye. If he was steppin' out, he was damn good at keeping it under wraps." She picked up the picture again and pressed it to her lips. "Those Thursday visits are just another part of Gramps's story that didn't belong to me exclusively. Just ask your uncle, baby. He'll tell you."

Gams breathed in, and within minutes, she was passed out on the couch, still holding that picture in her hand. I got up and grabbed her a blanket from the linen closet down the hall, then spread it over her and kissed her on the cheek before making my way down to the media room where Uncle Lem was watching the Rockets put a clinic on the Clippers.

"Wassup Unc?" I walked in and patted him on the shoulder over the back of the red, leather recliner he was sitting in.

"Aye." He tipped his chin up, taking a sip of coffee from his favorite coffee cup as I rounded the row of leather recliners and took a seat in the one next to him.

"Look like these boys might be tryna do somethin' this year." He glanced at me then took his eyes back to the big screen we'd mounted on the wall in front of us.

"Yeah, if they can stay healthy." I returned. "Hardin can't do it by himself." I looked up at the screen after Hardin sunk a three and backed away putting up that cheerio.

"I'on't know. That boy cold!" Unc popped the armrest. With less than a minute left in the fourth quarter, the Rockets were looking to rack up a dub, holding the lead by thirteen points.

"Yeah, I guess." I laughed, reclining the seat through the last few seconds of the game before I built up the nerve to bring up why I'd come in.

"Unc, can I pull ya ear for a minute?"

He tipped his head up and took another swig from his coffee. Uncle Lem wasn't a man of many words.

"The other night, when we were dropping ole girl off..."

"Joletta. Don't act like you ain't got her name committed to memory!" He laughed and I couldn't help laughing too.

"Yeah, *her*." I shook my head. "Anyway, her grandmother had a picture of Gramps in her phot album. You know anything about that?" I asked.

Uncle Lem's eyes took on the same look they'd taken on when he delivered Gramps's eulogy. I'd never forget that look. He told me himself that the worst responsibility his older brother had ever passed down to him was that, but he couldn't say no. Gramps had given him so much, he felt obligated to do whatever he asked. I wouldn't know the full extent of what Uncle Lem meant until he sat beside me in that red leather recliner and disclosed a secret that not even Gams was willing to share. What Gramps and Uncle Lem had was something most folks only wished for. They were way more than just brothers. They were ride or die best friends.

"I'm only gone tell you this cause you asking for it as a grown man." He started. "But I don't want no sympathy for it, and I won't accept no judgment, cause I'm better off and have been since November first, nineteen eighty."

I looked at him and nodded my head. Didn't need to mention that that date was exactly four years before the day I was born cause Uncle Lem was a flesh and blood archive of everybody's birthday that he'd ever known. I did feel like I needed to brace myself, though. The way he was going into this conversation reminded me a lot of the day that Gams and Gramps told me my Mama wasn't coming to pick me up after I went home with them the night our home went up in flames. I was only six years old, but that conversation changed the course of my life as I knew it. Couldn't even gain closure by seeing her lying in a coffin due to the condition of her remains. I lived out the rest of my childhood pretending it was all just a dream, and that Mama would be on the other side of the door every time somebody rang the doorbell.

"I used to be on drugs, nephew." He said, breaking me out of my thoughts. "And I ain't talkin bout no weed. I'm talkin dark alley, no sleep for seven days straight, selling the wheels off my car and *walking* to the dope house, crack cocaine."

Uncle Lem had a way with words that would have you laughing at shit that wasn't supposed to be funny. And that's exactly what I did. Luckily, so did he.

"It's funny now, but it was a damn shame then." He continued. "Anyway, I'd been out there for, hell, I don't know, maybe five or six years. Ain't nobody from the family knew where I was. And I know they was lookin', cause that's just the kinda family we got, ya know."

I nodded yes and crossed my arms. Unc had me pulled into this story, tryna guess the damn ending.

"Like I told you, I'd sold the wheels off my car." He kept going. "I ain't making that up. I sold a set of barely used tires for five dollars a piece, then sobered up a few hours after I hit that bump and realized, I needed to drive my black ass back to my old lady's house clear across the other side of I-45." Unc's hands went up in the air like he was reliving that day all over again. His face scrunched up like he was mad at himself, wishing he could take that fool shit back.

"So what'd you do?" I asked, in a hurry to get to the good part. He leaned forward and rested his elbows on his thighs, legs as long as mine with just a few more miles on em.

"I started walkin'." He said, looking sideways at me. "Made it about three miles up the road and had about ten more to go before your grandpa pulled over on the side of the road and threw my ass in the back seat!"

He sat straight up and clapped his hands together. I'm sitting there tuned in like I'm watching a damn movie. "You gotta be shittin me!?" I said.

"Right hand to the man!" He put his right hand up. "And I done went in circles with your grandma for the past thirty-eight years about this, but I swear, it wasn't nobody but God that made me sell those tires that night."

I almost fucking screamed. This dude had to be outta his mind if he thought God had anything to do with him selling the tires off his car to buy crack. I had to know why he thought that. So, I asked "Unc, you playing right?" I hissed out a chuckle, arms unfolded and planted on the armrests on either side of me.

"Hell naw." He squeaked. "If I hadn't sold those tires that night, I woulda drove home. And the route drivin' wasn't the same as the route walkin'. Avis woulda never crossed my path if I was on forty-five and he was on the feeder. We woulda been two ships passin' in the night, and worse than that, my ass might not be alive to tell you this story right now."

I could hardly digest the realness in that statement. Couldn't believe that Uncle Lem had ever been addicted to anything but coffee, and sure as hell couldn't imagine Gramps combing the hood looking for him. It's crazy how much shit people can keep from you for so long, but I didn't question their motives. Just took his confession for what it was and kept it in my chest where he asked me to keep it.

We sat in the room for a little while longer after he told me that Gramps had taken him to a drug rehab center the Monday after finding him walking down the feeder road. He said that after being clean and sober for ninety days, the center allowed him a pass to leave for the day every Thursday, but only under Gramps's supervision. He told me that on that day, every week, rain sleet or snow, he and Gramps used to load up the fruit truck and deliver fruit to the neighborhood where he used to buy crack. Said Gramps was determined to help him repay a debt to the community he'd likely stolen from to support his habit, by giving them some form of nourishment, and in turn redeeming himself.

That had to be the most poetic shit I'd ever heard in my life, and made perfect sense in the simplest way. By the time me and Uncle Lem left to turn it in for the night, I felt so full of good energy, I couldn't even go to sleep.

Lying awake in my bed while the rain poured down outside my window, my mind went to the one person it'd been going to every night for the past week. I wondered if she remembered my Gramps too. If she'd benefited from the weekly fruit truck visits that I had no idea about. Crazy things started running through my head about how maybe our encounter wasn't so random at all. That maybe this cosmic draw I was experiencing had been planted by my grandfather from wherever he was. The man always told me he'd take care of me until it was time for me to take care of myself. I couldn't help but think maybe the old man wasn't done.

Five

Jo

She claimed not to be, but Aunt Janine was more like her sister—
my mother—than anybody. Selfish, inconsiderate, and
opportunistic as fuck. She never did anything for anybody if it
didn't benefit her in some kind of way. Though nothing bad had
happened, I was still pissed at her for leaving Mama alone that
night a week prior. And she was fumbling all over herself tryna get
back in my good graces. Not because she gave a fuck about me or
Mama, but because she needed the little change I was giving her,
so she could run off to the gambling shack.

I'd picked up three gigs with Nessa that week, and had enough
money put away to take care of my portion of the bills and pay her
back for the week I'd missed. She was something like a blood
hound when it came to money. Seemed like she'd sniffed out my
earnings from her apartment on the other side of town.

"We already ate breakfast, Aunt Janine. Your envelope's on
the kitchen table." I yelled to her from the living room to the
kitchen, where she was pretending to give a damn if her mother ate

or not.

"Excuse me?" She came out of the kitchen with her hands on her hips, stale wig sitting on top of her round head smelling like cigarette smoke.

"We ate." I repeated, digging my elbow into one of the flat pillows on Mama's sofa, propping my cheek on a fist while I flipped through the TV channels. "Modesty's not your best trait, Auntie. I know you ain't here to check on Mama. Your money's in the envelope. Sorry for the late payment." I rattled off.

She rolled her eyes, full lips curved into a smirk, then switched her wide ass over to the kitchen table to snatch up the envelope.

"You're rude just like your Mama." She said.

"And you're selfish just like your sister." I shot back. "And I'm done with school til January, so you don't have to worry about Mama."

"It's not a problem, Jo." She changed her tone. Probably had visions of money leaving her pocket book.

"Apparently, it was." I said. "You left her here alone. What if she woulda fell? What if she burned the damn house down?"

"Watch your mouth, Joletta Rene!" Mama's voice startled me coming from her end of the hallway, leaning on her walker. "And I'm not a baby. I don't need nobody watching me like one."

"I know you're not a baby, Mama." I shook my head. "But you're also not a spring chicken. And I don't appreciate her leaving you here alone when I'm paying her cash to be here."

"That cash was a week late and this envelope feels a little light if you're paying me interest." Aunt Janine said, shaking the envelope back and forth like the loan shark she was.

"*Interest*? Are you serious right now?" I squinted my eyes at her, sitting straight up on the couch, causing Mama to speed up here entry into the living room.

"Now y'all stop it." She said, eyes roving from me to Aunt Janine. "Ain't no need to be splitting hairs. I'm fine."

"I'm not splittin' nothin', Mama." I said. "It's bad enough I gotta pay her to do something she should be doing for free. Now she wants to charge interest? Pitiful." I stood from the sofa and rolled my eyes as I passed Aunt Janine in route to my bedroom to grab my purse.

"How much?" I came back out with my wallet in hand. "How much interest are you charging to watch over your own mother?"

"Rene, I said stop it. And I mean it." Mama shifted against her walker, voice raising a little which instantly made me feel guilty. But I had a point to make, a test to give, if you will. And if I knew my auntie the way I thought I did, she'd fail with flying colors.

"One hundred dollars." Aunt Janine said without hesitation, eyes fixed on my wallet like a moth to a flame.

"See!" I bucked my eyes at Mama then rolled them to Aunt Janine. "Here." I shoved the money in her direction. She almost broke her fingers snatching it from me.

"Thank you." She said, stuffing the money in her bra. "Mama, you need anything?" She adjusted her double D's to make sure the cash was secure.

"All I need is for you to get your selfish ass outta my house!" Mama looked up at her oldest daughter and shook her head before slowly heading into the living room, mumbling profanities under her breath.

"I'm not wrong." Aunt Janine said to me, clutching her money-filled envelope as if she thought I might take it back. "Don't nobody work for free, not even for their mother. You ain't gone play no guilt trip on me."

"Go home, Janine!" Mama yelled from the living room,

waiting for me to come and help her sit down. "Or to that damn gambling shack or wherever you running off to, to dodge that beer drinking husband of yours."

I rushed over to hold Mama from over the back of the couch as she eased down into her seat.

"And don't you give her another dime." Mama looked up at me over her shoulder. "Put that money in the bank somewhere. You gone need it to print them books."

"What books?" Aunt Janine asked with one hand on the doorknob and the other on her hip.

"The book she writin' about this family." Mama said. "You might know that if you asked her about more than a got damn paycheck."

"Am I gonna be in it?" Aunt Janine looked at me and asked.

"Hell yeah you gone be in it!" Mama answered for me. "In all the worst parts, I'm sure. Now get on outta here." She threw a hand up in the air then turned back around and reached for the remote I'd left on the cushion next to her.

"Well I love you too, Mama." Aunt Janine curved her lips, pushing the door open, then stepping back in. "Um, somebody's out there." She said.

"Probably for the neighbors. We're not expecting company." I said.

"Nah, you might wanna come look at this." Her eyes widened.

I left Mama and hurried to the door, and my bottom lip almost hit the floor when I saw what was outside in front of our house. Something from my childhood that I hadn't seen for at least fifteen years. A big red truck with fruits and vegetables painted along the side. *Paul's Freshest* fruit truck!

"Mama, I think… I think *Fruit Man's* out here." I said, still puzzled. "I thought you said he die?" I questioned.

"Nobody knew for sure if he died or not, Rene. We just assumed, cause he stopped coming around." She looked over her shoulder. "Bring me my wheels. I wanna see this for myself."

"I'll get it." Aunt Janine offered.

"I'm not paying you." I noted.

"And I'm not *asking* you to." She rolled her eyes, brushing past me in route to Mama's room to retrieve her wheelchair.

I stepped out onto the porch as other neighbors did the same—some old enough to remember the last time the *Fruit Man* had visited the neighborhood. If it was him, I'd be surprised to see someone his age still taking on such a task. He usually had a guy along helping him—his brother I'm assuming due to the striking resemblance—but they didn't look that far apart in age, so this'd be a task for him as well. The sound of Mama's wheelchair being rolled down the hallway took my attention away from the fruit truck and back inside where Mama had scooted to the edge of the sofa. I rushed over to help Aunt Janine get her in the chair, then rolled her up to the front door so she could see the big red truck that had brightened so many of her days.

"Can't believe that old thang is still runnin'!" She laughed, shoulders jumping. "Ole *Fruit Man*!" She settled back in her chair, wearing a suspicious smile that, for some reason, made me nervous.

I stood behind Mama's chair, holding onto the handles as I looked down and pushed my foot on the breaks behind her wheels to lock them in place. What I saw when I looked up was nothing short of beautiful. I didn't even realize my mouth was hanging open, until he put a finger under his bottom lip, mocking me.

"Wassup? Heard y'all could use some fresh fruit around here!"

Skoby's smile was nearly as bright as the sun, muscled chest rising and falling beneath a red *Nike* T shirt as he breathed, probably unnoticeable to my grandmother and aunt, because they hadn't sank their nails into it while screaming their way through an orgasm, or rested their head upon it and drifted off to sleep.

"We can *always* use anything you're bringing!" Aunt Janine flirted, batting her eyes and primping that raggedy ass wig. "You need some help?" She offered. And I was certain she wasn't talking about fruit.

"No ma'am. I brought some help with me." He replied wearing a handsome smile. And I felt relieved for reasons I wasn't willing to admit out loud.

He stepped in closer and grabbed ahold of Mama's hand, sending her high cheekbones into a grin. "You doing alright, Mama Jo? I got back as fast as I could." He said.

"I've been fine, Skoby. Good to see that old truck again." She replied cheerfully, looking past Skoby at the fruit truck.

"Really? You mean to tell me you're happier to see that truck than you are to see me?" He teased. This nigga was really laying it on thick for my grandma.

"Well, I didn't say all that!" She softened her smile, taking her eyes off the truck and back up to the brown eyes of the charming stranger who was making it his business to be in my vicinity no matter what lengths he had to travel to get there.

"Well that's good to hear." He nodded, giving her hand a squeeze before letting it go. "I know these folks don't know me out here. I was wondering if maybe y'all could help me get the word out? We got a truck full of fresh produce, and we can't leave until everybody gets what they need."

So wrapped up in their friendly interaction, I didn't even notice Mama's eyes on me until Aunt Janine cleared her throat to snap me out of it.

"Hmm hmm!" She grunted. "I think my niece knows this neighborhood better than the back of her hand."

"She do." Mama added. "You heard the man, Rene. Help him get the word out!" She winked at me, and there was nothing I could do, standing there all exposed and put on the spot. What the hell did he think he was doing?

"Fine." I gave a fake smile, rolling my eyes at Skoby while Mama was looking off down the sidewalk at the few neighbors who were looking on but hesitant to approach the big red truck.

Skoby had run off to grab something from the truck, then returned to my side as I proceeded down the block, holding out a stack of post-card sized flyers.

"Hey, I had these printed up." He said, breathing dangerously close to my ear. "Thought maybe we could pass em out."

"What are you doing?" I asked, quickly approaching the next house on the block where our neighbor and her two small sons were standing on the porch, looking in our direction with curiosity.

"I'm giving away fresh produce. You ain't hear me when I—"

"I'm not talking about the damn fruit truck, Skoby!" I cut him off, stopping in my tracks since the family on the porch was still tuned in. "I'm talking about *this*. You showing up in front of my house unannounced when I specifically asked you not to come around here again."

"Oh, I see. You think this is about you?" He turned to look me straight in the face, the smell of sweat mixed with his cologne almost took me to my knees. "Well it's not, Princess."

"I'm not a fucking Princess!"

"Apparently not."

"What is that supposed to mean?"

"It means you're ungrateful." He returned, giving me as much attitude as I was giving him.

I had no rebuttal, choosing instead to turn forward and

continue walking.

"Jo." He called my name, still standing where I'd left him.

I didn't respond or slow down.

"Jo, I know you heard me!" He called again, and I still didn't respond.

"Fine." I heard his footsteps approaching, and was relieved. As much as I'd pretended I didn't want the man around, his presence literally woke up my insides.

"Are you used to be chased?" He asked, quickly closing the gap between us. "Cause this shit can get old fa—"

"Hey Shalonda!" I cut him off, greeting my neighbor and snatching a flyer from Skoby's hands. "I don't know if you remember the fruit truck that used to come around here, but it's making a comeback. This is Skoby, the…"

"Owner. I'm the owner." He stepped up next to me. "Nice to meet you, Shalonda. If you need anything, just go on down to the truck and let the workers know. We got boxes and carts if you need em."

He shook Shalonda's hand and her lite brown cheeks reddened with a smile.

"He's single too, girl!" I added with internal hesitance.

And he smiled at her. This mother fucker had the nerve to smile at another woman right in my face when he was probably still savoring the taste of my pussy on his tongue. Granted, I brought that shit on myself. But still.

Fucking *still!*

"Nice meeting you, Shalonda." He shook her hand again, then gave both her boys hi-fives and got their names before fanning out a hand for us to continue down the sidewalk.

"That was cute." He said, walking slower since his legs were longer. "The old hook up game. That was real nice."

"Just tryna help a brother out." I looked up beside me at him.

"Thanks, but I'm good." He chuckled.

"What, you don't like Shalonda?" I asked, looking ahead of me because I didn't need his expression giving away any truth that might hurt my feelings.

"She aight." I saw his shoulders shrug from the corner of my eye. "Not my type though."

I sat with the question for all of three seconds before I asked, "What is your type?" and felt stupid as hell as soon as the words left my lips.

He didn't respond, and I wasn't surprised. He owed me for giving him so much shit. But I wasn't gonna press. It would go against everything I'd said up to this point. If Skoby wanted to play this game, he was gonna have to find somebody else to play with.

But I hoped he didn't.

"Wait a minute, is that? Nah, can't be." He squinted. Something or someone down the sidewalk had caught his eye.

"What? Somethin wrong?" I asked, looking at the side of his head then back down the sidewalk to see if I'd missed something.

"Nothin'. It's just, that little girl, she looks familiar. I'm sure it's not who I think it is though."

"Well, we could walk down there and find out." I offered, part nosey part curious. "Or we could just wait for her to crash into us, cause now she's running."

"Daddy!" A little brown girl with hair almost as big as her came barreling down the sidewalk in our direction.

Skoby's eyes lit up like Christmas lights as the girl made it to him and wrapped her little arms around his thigh. "I knew that was you, Daddy!" She squeezed him tight, looking up into his eyes.

He pulled her arms from around him and went down into a squat, bracing her little face between his big hands. "Who you with, Krissi?" He asked in the sweetest most concerned tone.

"Miss Iris." The little girl said. "Is that your girlfriend? She's pretty!" She looked up at me.

Skoby took a deep breath, pulled her head in and kissed her forehead, then stood up and grabbed ahold of her hand. "Show me where Miss Iris lives, Krissi." He demanded without answering her question.

"I'm sorry, Jo. You mind passing out the rest of these? I gotta take care of this." He said, handing me the rest of the flyers.

"Sure. I got it. Go ahead."

I watched the both of them make their way down the sidewalk. Krissi kept looking back at me smiling, little pink tennis shoes hitting the pavement with the same stride as her daddy. I'd pegged Skoby for a lot of things; a dope boy maybe. A serial womanizer for sure. Even considered making him a routine late-night creep before better judgement told me not to. But I'd never pegged him for being anybody's daddy. Guess there really was more to this man than meets the eye.

Skoby

"Three days? Where she been for three days? She didn't call me about this. This is my daughter, man! I think I should at least know who she's with when she ain't with me."

The heavy-set stranger whose house smelled like spaghetti didn't seem at all concerned about how pissed I was. But she should've been. I didn't play when it came to most shit, especially not my daughter. Her mama cared more about hitting the damn streets than she did about being with her child. And I'd been letting shit go for the sake of peace. But this time she'd taken it too far. Literally fell off the fucking map and left my baby with somebody I'd never met in my damn life.

"She said she was going on a cruise." The lady—Miss Iris— explained, wiping her hands off on an apron that had more stains on it than I was comfortable with. "It won't do you no good to call." She added. "Ain't no reception on those cruise ships."

I can't believe this bitch went on a fucking cruise and left my baby with a stranger when she could've called me. I thought to myself, but wouldn't dare say that out loud in front of Krissi.

"Well how were you supposed to get in touch with her if something happened to Krissi?" I asked with Krissi's arms wrapped around my thigh, thumb plopped in her mouth, even though I'd been telling her since she was old enough to listen to stop sucking her thumb.

"Krissi's fine." Miss Iris replied. "She stays here all the time and ain't nothin' happened to her yet. Ain't that right, Miss Krissi!?" She smiled down at my baby, and I didn't doubt that Krissi felt safe with the woman. I just wasn't okay with my baby staying somewhere other than with me or my family when her stupid ass mama was outta pocket.

"Well that's a good thing." I reached down and pulled Krissi's thumb outta her mouth. She wasn't a titty baby, so she didn't fight me on it. "And I don't mean no disrespect, Miss Iris, but Krissi's coming with me."

Krissi's eyes lit up. She was always happy when I came to scoop her up. Due to the hustle and bustle I was dealing with, taking over *Paul's Freshest* around the same time Krissi was born, I'd only been awarded joint custody, getting to pick her up every other weekend. Grams kept telling me I needed to get that shit amended. Guess this was the kick in the ass that I'd needed.

"And I don't mean no disrespect either, but Kerri doesn't pay me until she gets back. And I doubt she'll be paying me for a baby that ain't here."

"How much?" I returned without flinching. Seemed like money was always at the center of every relationship Kerri ever had.

"Five hundred." She said. I could see the dollar signs floating over her head.

I pulled out my wallet and flipped out six crisp Benjamins, then handed them to her and walked out with my baby, waving goodbye to Miss Iris who hadn't looked up from her earnings.

"You hungry?" I looked down at my baby. A head full of kinky coils crowned her head. She looked so much like me it was scary. Didn't get nothing from Kerri but her eyes.

"Yeah." She nodded, big Hazel eyes looking up at me like I was the king of the world.

"Uh uh. What are you supposed to say?" I asked, cause she knew better.

"Yes sir!" She grinned.

"That's right. And why?" I pressed, knowing she was fully capable of retaining information. She was probably calculating how long it would be before she could tell her mama I'd taken her from the babysitter.

"Cause good girls have good grades and good manners!" She recited the words I'd been repeating to her since her first day of pre-K.

"You got it." I raised my palm and we connected for a hi-five, just in time to come in contact with Jo, who'd apparently been beating the block and handed out all but three of the flyers.

"Hey! Y'all good?" She asked, glancing down at Krissi, then back up at me.

"Yeah. We good." I answered, surprised to see her so welcoming but knowing it was more for my daughter's sake than mine. "I don't think I properly introduced you two. Jo, this is my baby girl, Krissi. Krissi this is my... this is Jo." I swallowed. I didn't know how else to introduce her.

Jo extended a slim, pretty hand to Krissi who shook it as hard as she could, because I'd also taught my baby that honest people gave firm handshakes.

"I like your hair." Krissi said, brown cheeks fluffing. "It looks like mine. *See!*" She twirled her fingers through her kinks.

"It sure does." Jo smiled. "And I think your hair's pretty too!" She winked, then brought her eyes back up to me.

"Umm, I finished handing out the flyers." She spoke as if she wasn't sure what tone to take with me. "I think almost everybody got what they needed. A few folks don't want it if it ain't fried so, there's that." She shrugged, pretty lips curving to the side.

"Cool." I nodded. "And thanks for... for helping out. I appreciate it."

"Not a problem." She folded her arms across her chest, standing in awkward silence for a moment that seemed to last an hour. Even in jeans and a T shirt, Jo was easily the prettiest woman I'd ever seen.

Then Krissi blurted "We're gonna go eat. You wanna come?"

The look of shock on Jo's face was almost enough to make me bust out laughing. I figured I'd save her since I knew she didn't wanna go and might not have the heart to kill my little girl's spirit.

"Krissi, I'm sure Jo has other stuff to do." I said. "Maybe some other time."

"Yeah, I'm... I am a little busy, sweetie. I'm sorry." She looked down at Krissi apologetically.

"Doing what?" My baby was persistent for a four-year old.

"Umm… I have to… to help out my grandma." Jo reached far and hard for an answer. "She doesn't get around well and she needs me for some things."

"Well, we can help her before we go. Come on!" Krissi pulled at my hand, looking up at me when I didn't move. "Daddy, let's go." She demanded. "We gotta go help Jo's grandma so we can go eat."

"Krissi—"

"It's fine." Jo cut me off. "She's right. We can all help my grandma. Krissi's a problem solver!" She smiled, and I didn't know where she was going with this.

We made our way down the sidewalk back to Mama Jo's where the workers I'd brought with me from the factory finished loading up the truck. I went over to let them know that I'd be staying for a bit and that they could go ahead without me. I'd just call Uncle Lem to come scoop me and Krissi.

By the time I wrapped up, Jo and my baby girl had made it inside and Krissi was standing on a footstool washing her hands at the kitchen sink next to Jo. Mama Jo was sitting in her respective spot in the living room. Jo's aunt had left for whatever she had to do, and it felt cozy and comfortable in the space. Like something from a show on TGIF.

"Young man, you sure did make my day!" Mama Jo smiled so big it almost made me blush when I rounded the sofa to take a seat next to her. "All those babies running down the street with bunches of bananas and bags of apples. You don't see that around here no more. Nothin but hot chips and sodas."

"Yeah. Jo told me." I said. "I didn't think I was gonna get rid of one grape, if I'm being honest, Mama Jo. I don't know how my grandpa did it."

"It's all in the truck, baby." She nodded. "You see something that bright and colorful pulling up in your neighborhood, you're gonna break your neck getting to it. And I sure hope this ain't one and done." She patted my thigh. "This neighborhood could use somethin' good passin' through every once in a while."

I took a deep breath, taking her words seriously and wondering if I'd be able to keep up with this thing. To tell the truth, I don't know if I was doing it more for Gramps's legacy or as a means to get closer to Jo. Either cause would be beneficial to my life. Of course with one requiring a little more effort and a shit load of patience. And even then, I couldn't be sure she'd be receptive.

"I'm gonna try my best." I said in response, meaning it more than she probably knew. With her granddaughter in the background showing my daughter, a complete stranger, how to wash dishes, a little hope had been sparked for the kid.

Six

Jo

It hadn't rained a drop all day. But as we approached the entry to his gated community, the got damn sky opened up. I wanted to ask what the hell we were doing here, but after overhearing him talking on the phone, it dawned on me that when Krissi was asking for a specific meal from *Gams*, she wasn't referring to a restaurant. She was talking about her great-grandmother. Never one to spoil a kid's spirit, I went along with the little game and kept my mouth shut. Uncle Lem pulled up to a covered area alongside the mini-mansion, then climbed out to open the door for me and Krissi while Skoby hopped out on the other side.

"Sorry for getting you out in this weather, Unc." He slapped hands with his uncle, more than likely leaving him a huge tip because apparently, that's the kind of shit he did.

Within seconds, he'd joined me and Krissi on our way down a short, pebbled path that ended at a wide-open tall, blue door with the smell of something savory swimming from it.

"Gams makes the best sweet potato casserole in the world!" Krissi pressed her little hands together, so excited I thought her cheeks might burst. "And she doesn't make me eat my chicken. Do you like chicken, Jo?" Her little eyes looked up at me. I'd never seen a little girl who looked so much like her father.

"Actually, I do." I replied, catching Skoby peeping our conversation as he led the way to the door. "Especially fried chicken. It's my favorite!" I said excitedly, praying that there was some chicken being fried alongside that sweet potato casserole. It'd be the least he could offer for tricking me into returning to his house.

As we approached the open door behind Skoby, my breath was completely taken away by what I was seeing and smelling. It seemed like such an awkward placement for a kitchen in a space this big. It was almost its on section, fully equipped with patio furniture right outside.

I allowed myself to imagine myself eating out there, whether it be alone, or with Skoby. Either would've been just fine. I must've been wearing the awe all over my face, cause when I stepped into the kitchen, the beautiful older lady responsible for the aroma quickly brought her eyes to me and smiled.

"It's a lot ain't it?" She laughed, and all I could do was nod my head.

"I'm sorry, it's beautiful." I managed to form words, eyes traveling up to the highest point of the ceiling where a stream of horizontal lights hung, spanning from one end of the wall to the other.

"Gams, this is Jo. She likes fried chicken. You can give her mine!" Krissi rattled that off with her arm roped around Gams leg, plopping her thumb in her mouth when she finished.

"Well I'm glad to see somebody has manners around here." Gams teased, cutting her eyes at Skoby. "And get that thumb outta your mouth before you ruin your teeth." She reached down and gently swatted Krissi's hand.

"Go wash ya hands, Krissi." Skoby commanded, leaning against the countertop.

Krissi ran off down the hallway in a hurry, giggling all the way.

"Sorry for losing my manners." He said, eyes jotting between me and Gams. "Jo, this is my grandmother, Julia. But we call her Gams. Gams, this is Jo. She's a…"

"Friend." I stepped in. I'd already watched him struggle through that introduction with Krissi. I couldn't watch him do it again.

"Friend?" She widened her eyes at me.

"Yes, *friend*." I repeated, leaving no room for further reading.

"Hmmf!" She huffed, wearing a smile that had bullshit written all over it. "Bee ain't brought a *friend* home since he made Krissi. I hope you ain't that kinda friend."

"I'm not." I said before I knew it. And the look on Skoby's face almost made me feel bad.

Almost.

I hadn't asked him to bring me here, so whatever he got was on him.

"Well it's nice to meet you, Jo. I hope you didn't eat before you came." She slanted her eyes at Skoby then turned back around to face the stove. "Make yourself at home. I'm almost done in here."

"You need help with anything?" I asked. Mama's voice was in my ear threatening to whoop my ass if I didn't.

Gams almost looked stunned, like I'd said something in Spanish and she wasn't sure how to respond.

"I'm sorry, did I say something wrong?" I couldn't help but ask due to the long pause.

"Oh baby, no!" She planted a hand on my shoulder. "I'm just not used to Skoby's *friends* offering a helping hand around here. You know your way around a Koolaid pitcher?" She asked, and a smile sprang from my lips that almost hurt.

Skoby was still holding his spot against the island, shaking his head and chuckling at his grandma's shenanigans.

"Lead me to the sugar and I got you!" I smashed a fist into my palm and slid sideways to the sink to wash my hands.

Wearing a smile bigger than his head, Skoby retrieved all the utensils and ingredients needed to make Koolaid. They had no idea what they'd gotten themselves into, challenging a girl from the hood with making the *hoodest* drink known to man. I'd literally trained for this moment my whole life. I was about to blow their got damned minds.

The dinner table had been set, but there were only four place settings. Uncle Lem was pretty reclusive, but I'd at least expected to see him for dinner. Nobody else seemed put off by his absence but I'd noticed him disappearing down the hallway shortly after we came in, and my curiosity was getting the best of me. I wasn't used to being in a house so big that a single person could disappear down a hallway without me knowing exactly where he went.

"Is your uncle gonna eat?" I asked Skoby as we took our seats.

Gams insisted on bringing our food to the table and I didn't take her for the kind of woman you wanted to argue with.

"Yeah, just not in here." He leaned to the side and answered. "Uncle Lem's got a smacking problem and it drives Gams crazy."

"Are you serious?"

"Dead serious. Dude could wake the dead when he chews." Skoby shook his head. "I mean I can tolerate it, but Gams got a short fuse."

"I like the way Uncle Lemon chews his food." Krissi added, looking up from her coloring sheet. "It's musical." She shrugged, looking right back down at the sheet.

"I'm sorry. That's just... that's crazy. What's he gonna do, eat in the back like an animal or somethin'?" The whole thing just bothered me too much to look past.

"He's in the media room." Skoby pointed in the direction of the hallway I'd seen Uncle Lem disappear down earlier. "You can take him his plate if you want. He ain't gonna bite you."

"I think I will." I pushed my chair back and stood from the tall backed seat I'd been sitting in.

"Can I come?" Krissi's big eyes came up from her coloring sheet again. I looked to Skoby for approval, and when he nodded yes, me and Krissi went into the kitchen to grab Uncle Lem's plate from Gams.

Surprisingly, she didn't put up a fuss. Apparently Krissi'd pulled this same thing a time or two, and Gams didn't care how Uncle Lem got his plate, as long as she didn't have to hear him eat it.

"Uncle Lemon, we got your food!" Krissi cheerfully announced, after leading me down a lit hallway where a huge media room was at the end.

Uncle Lem was sitting on the first of four rows of cinema themed recliners, watching an old western movie with a piping hot cup of coffee sitting in a cup holder in the arm of the seat.

"Hey, I hope we didn't disturb your movie." I said, stepping up beside him, holding a hot plate of fried chicken wings, sweet potato casserole, mustard greens, and a wide slice of cornbread. "This is a nice set-up." I observed as Krissi climbed in the seat next to Uncle Lem, pushing a button on the side of the seat that let out the foot rest.

"Got plenty of room if you don't mind a little noise!" He smiled, flipping out an eating tray from the side of the chair and motioning for me to sit his dinner plate on top of it.

"You know what, I don't mind a little noise at all." I smiled. "Lemme go grab my plate. Krissi, you eating in here too?" She nodded yes, pulling out her eating tray, and I hurried off down the hallway to grab our plates.

It was a little awkward at first, leaving Skoby and Gams at the dinner table while me and Krissi ate with Uncle Lem. Listening to her clap out an improvised song to the rhythm of him smacking had to be the funniest shit I'd ever witnessed in my thirty years on earth. I'm sure Skoby wanted to join us, but it might've hurt Gams's feelings if everybody left her sitting at the dinner table alone. It would've given her a taste of her own medicine though. I couldn't believe Uncle Lem had been sitting in that media room by himself every night. A little smacking never killed nobody.

After dinner and dessert, Gams gave Krissi a bath and put her to bed before retiring to bed herself. The rain outside hadn't slacked up at all, and I needed to go home, but didn't feel right having Uncle Lem driving in those conditions. Skoby returned from the restroom while I was sitting on the couch. We hadn't talked too much outside the company of his family, and it seemed like he didn't know what to say now that we were alone.

"It's pretty bad out there." He said, sexy fucking lips trying their damndest to entice me.

"Yeah. I was thinking about just calling a Lyft." I said, pulling out my phone. "Wouldn't want Uncle Lem getting stuck out in this storm."

"And you think a Lyft'll be safer?" He asked, house slippers flopping against the hardwood floors.

"For him, yeah." I bucked my eyes.

"True. But that's not what I meant. Why don't you stay here tonight? We'll get you home first thing in the morning."

"Skoby?"

"Skoby what? I got a guest room." He pointed up the stairs. "I swear, I'm not tryna get your booty, man." He chuckled. "It's nasty out there. Just tryna help."

I mulled it over in my head. The thought of being in his house but not in his bed almost made me sick to my stomach. Of course, I wouldn't admit that out loud, but it was still a thing and I hated myself for it.

Finally, after much deliberation, I accepted the offer after calling Mama to make sure she was okay, and finding out that Aunt Janine had picked her up and taken her to her place to ride out the storm. That guilt trip Mama threw at her earlier must've really taken root. I could count on one hand how many times Mama had been to the home Aunt Janine shared with her alcoholic ass husband.

In any event, I was Skoby's for the night—company that is. And he set me up in a nice guest room on the opposite end of the hallway from the room he'd shared with me weeks before. Along with a set of soft white bath towels, he handed me one of his t-shirts that fell just above my knees to sleep in. I unfolded the T shirt after washing up in the beautifully decorated en suite bathroom, and a pair of black panties fell out onto the sink that were exactly the right size. Puzzled, I stared at them for a minute, hesitant to put them on because I wasn't sure if they had a prior owner. Then it dawned on me, when I'd left his house with bacon in tow that day, I'd neglected to locate my panties.

I pulled them up to my nose and the smell of Suavitel liquid fabric softener kissed my nostrils like a morning at the laundromat. I don't know what was more surprising, the fact that he'd kept my panties or the fact that he'd had them cleaned. Either way I was impressed. Another thing I'd have to keep to myself.

After dressing myself, I toed out of the bathroom, and fell back on a bed that wasn't as big as Skoby's but was equally as comfy. I doubted these bed sheets were available in stores. They felt like heaven against my bare skin. Mind going a thousand miles a minute, I pulled my phone off the nightstand and opened the Windows app. It was times like this when I couldn't share my thoughts that I needed to jot them down for safe keeping.

He's so close to me

Way too close

Closer than I'd allow

If he was asking permission

He's so close to me

Way too close

Closer than I can stand

But I'm not asking for distance

A short poem was all I had in the chamber, and it still didn't help my mind to shut off. After lying on my back watching the ceiling fan spin for thirty minutes, I finally decided that enough was enough. I climbed outta bed and walked over to the bedroom door, looking down the hallway in the direction of Skoby's room. I couldn't see if there was a light on from under his door. That room was so tightly sealed it could turn day into night. Throwing caution to the wind, I left the guest room and headed over to his, praying with every step that he was still awake too. I'd be mortified if I knocked and woke the man from his sleep. Cause what would I do then, turn around and run?

Tap Tap. I stood at his door, tugging at the hem of the T shirt to try and make it longer.

"Come in." He said, voice clear and wide awake.

"Hey. Did I wake you?" I pushed the door open and asked anyway, peeping in to find him lying there with the covers up to his waist, bare abs and chest ripped and tatted with an arm tucked behind his head and a book in his hand.

"Nah, I was up." He glanced over at me, then closed the book and laid it on the nightstand. "You alright?"

"Yeah, I'm... I'm good. Just couldn't sleep." I stood near the door. Flashbacks of the things he'd done to me in that bed, on top of that dresser, and against the far wall near his window, made me hesitant to move any further. "This place is huge."

"I know." He nodded with a smile. "Been here almost two years and I still ain't used to it. You can sit down. I don't bite." He patted the space next to him.

"That's a damn lie!" I smirked, stepping in and pulling the door closed behind me, nipples beading at the thought of him capturing them between his teeth again.

He laughed and adjusted himself to make space as I padded over to the bed and sat on top of his crisp, white comforter. Chills ran down my spine in response to his scent. Hairs raised on the back of my neck when he looked at me.

"What?" I shrugged, eyes ballooning, trying hard not to blush.

"I didn't say nothin'!" He chuckled. "You're acting strange though."

"Strange how?"

"Like you've never been in my bed before. Or against that wall. Or bent over that dresser. It's cool, Jo. You can relax. I'll keep my dick in my shorts."

And why did the simple mention of his dick send moisture pooling between my legs?

"Listen, if we're gonna keep this friendly, you gotta refrain from mentioning that thing." I said, scooting back and flipping my legs up on the bed, sitting beside him and pushing my back against the tufted headboard that had been a soft place for my head to press against while he was fucking me from behind.

"What, you mean my dick?" He curled those sexy black lips, pointing at his crotch.

"Yes, your *dick*!" I rolled my eyes. "What were you reading?" I quickly changed the subject, praying he wasn't reading erotica.

"This book Gams bought for me a few years back. *Chicken Soup for a Man's Soul*." He picked the thick book up and handed it to me. "Good shit in there." He said as I opened it and flipped through the pages.

"Any good advice?" I asked, peeping up from the book.

"Nah. Mostly just stories about fathers and their kids. I wouldn't so much call it advice as it is things they expect people to relate to."

"*People*? Sounds like you're excluding yourself." I noted, handing the book back to him and soaking in the view of his back muscles flexing as he reached over to put it back on the nightstand.

"Alotta soft shit happens in that book." He returned to an upright position just in time to catch me looking.

"Oh, I see." I breathed out, canvasing the room in a moment of awkward silence.

I don't think Skoby knew the strength of his presence. Although I'd adamantly proclaimed how much I wanted to move on from whatever was happening between us, when I was near him, there was no denying the chemistry. He felt so good, even when I wasn't touching him. The sound of his voice made me wanna hand him my book of poems, so he could read them to me one by one.

I knew it wouldn't be long before I had to leave his bed and go back into that lonely room and stare at the ceiling fan until the sun came up. But I didn't want to. I wanted to lie next to him and wake up with the smell of him in my hair. I wanted to be wrapped up in his arms so bad, it hurt me that I'd made him think otherwise. Why was I like this? I didn't even know this man, but it felt like I did. Sitting beside him in the bed where we'd fucked like it was the end of the world, now pretending that we didn't wanna do it all over again, I felt like I knew him. Or at least I wanted to.

Jesus, I wanted to.

"You can sleep in here if you want." His smooth voice brought me out of my thoughts.

"I'm not sleepy." I said.

"Me either." He turned his head to the side and stared at me the way a man stares at a woman he wants to make love to.

"I'm not fucking you tonight, Skoby." I reminded him with a finger to his soft lips. "Not with your baby and your grandmother under the same roof."

"Who said I was tryna fuck, Joletta?" He grinned, licking his lips.

"Your eyes did. And don't call me that." I rubbed my hands up and down my arms.

"Why not?" He leaned to the side and rolled the covers down to pull them up over my legs.

"It's reserved." I replied, pulling the covers up the rest of the way up to my waist.

"For who?"

"You're nosey."

76

"I'm inquisitive."

"Same difference."

"You still haven't answered."

"And I'm not going to."

"Bet." He digressed. "But I don't know what we're supposed to do in here if we can't talk, sleep, or fuck."

I shook my head, eyes panning over to the window as the rain poured harder with every minute.

"We can talk. Just not about that."

"Aight, so what're we gonna talk about?" He put a hand behind his neck, turning his head to look at me again.

"I don't know, anything." I shrugged.

"Okay. Who's allowed to call you Joletta?" Here he was with the pressing.

"Are you deaf? I said no to that."

"That rule got swept off the bed when you said you'd talk about anything. Who is it, your boyfriend or somethin'?" I could hear a tinge of jealousy in his voice and decided to tap on that nerve.

"What if it is?" I smirked. "If my birth name is reserved for my boyfriend, would you respect that?"

"I'on't know. I like your name." That wasn't the answer I was expecting.

"What if he likes it too? You wouldn't give the man the respect he's due?" I folded my arms across my chest and looked him square in the eye.

He stroked his fingers down his beard and laughed at me before answering. "Any man that reserves the right to your birth name but can't call and check on you in the middle of a storm is hardly a boyfriend, mama." He said. "And if your eyes are saying what I think they're saying, that man don't even exist."

Fuck! He called my bluff.

"Whatever." Was my only rebuttal. "He could've called while I was in that dark ass room you put me in."

"And when he did, did you tell him you were sleeping under the roof of a man you'd had a smash and dash session with?" He rattled off.

"You don't have to answer that." He spoke before I could, flipping the covers down off of him and climbing out of the bed. "Come on, I wanna show you something."

"Skoby?"

"Seriously, I'm not on no sneak shit." He nodded before stepping into his closet and returning with a thick, black robe. "Put this on." He extended it in my direction as I hesitantly climbed out of bed and padded over to him.

"I swear, this better be a Christian activity or I'm waking Uncle Lem myself to drive me home." I slipped my arms into the robe that was at least two sizes too big.

"Oh, so you claiming my uncle now?" He huffed out a chuckle, slipping on a clean white T shirt that he'd taken from his dresser.

"I ate dinner with him, which is more than I can say for you and Gams." I rolled my eyes, still a little salty about the situation. Gams didn't strike me as the snotty type, but that was some real snotty shit.

"You got that situation all wrong," He defended, walking across the room to his bedroom door and pulling it open.

"How so? Y'all had him eating in a separate room like some kinda animal. Ain't too many ways to read that, sir." He stepped out and walked out behind him.

"People have their preferences, and I'm just tryna make sure my family's happy." His voice echoed off the walls and crown-molded ceilings as we neared the end of a long hallway that went in the opposite direction of the room I'd been sleeping in, and then down the stairs.

"So, you think Uncle Lem prefers to eat alone while you and Gams eat in the big dining room like slave masters or some shit? That sounds ridiculous." I quickened my steps to keep up with his long-legged strides.

"Not that it's any of your business," He slowed down, glancing back at me over his shoulder. "But I eat with Uncle Lem all the time. Gams ain't always here. And if Uncle Lem ain't eating, those two are as thick as thieves. She just can't stand to hear people smacking. We all got a thing that we can't tolerate and that's hers."

I shook my head and accepted that excuse, although it was a load of bullshit to me. "I guess." I said. "And where are you taking me?"

"Just keep walking." He said. He'd slowed his stride so that now we were walking side by side.

The house was so quiet you could hear a pin drop under the trickling from the manmade waterfall in the backyard flowing into the swimming pool. It was too nasty out to go for a dip, thunder clapping every few minutes and streaks of lightening dancing in the sky. As we passed the patio doors, I wondered what could possibly be more interesting on the property than that. At the end of another short hallway, clear on the other side of the house, was a tall set of double doors that I hadn't seen on either of my visits. Seemed odd enough, the way the space on that side of the house seemed so secluded from the rest. Figured it must be his office or something. Peace and quiet was probably essential for a business owner to keep his ducks in a row, even if he was selling something as simple as produce.

"Aight, this is it." He stopped before we got to the set of tall doors, standing in front of a smaller door that probably led to a room, and rested his long hand on the doorknob. "Close your eyes." He said.

"No." I returned. "I don't know what you're up to, but no."

"Fine." He surrendered faster than I'd expected, twisting the copper knob and pushing the door open in one swift motion.

And there it was.

Nothing.

A spacious room that could've functioned as anything from a master's bedroom, a small library, or even a den, sat empty with not even a picture hanging from the powder blue walls. In my mind, I questioned why he'd brought me here. Had he murdered six women and buried them behind those walls? Was I about to be victim number seven? I turned off my imagination long enough to notice that Skoby was watching me, adoring me even. He was weird in that way. Didn't seem to embarrass easily. When he saw something he liked, his eyes wouldn't let him lie.

"What is this?" I asked, echoes bouncing off all four walls.

"It's nothing." He said. "Gams had every room in this house decorated except for this one. Said she was waiting for a reason to fix it up."

"And you brought me here *because*?"

"I don't... I don't know." He shrugged, shoving his hands in his pockets. "Listen, I like you. And I don't know where all this is coming from, but I feel like... like I don't know what the fuck I'm doing."

"I'd have to agree with you on that!" I nodded, jokingly.

"This doesn't happen to me." He said, eyes low and sincere as he joined me at the center of the room. "Not knowing what to say. Not knowing what to do. I'm like, the king of communicating what

I want from a woman. Shit, from people period. But for some reason, that ain't the case with you."

"I think you're confused, Skoby." I backed away from him, turning around to walk toward a huge wall that would've been perfect if there was a window cut out. "You got exactly what you wanted from me. *We* got exactly what we wanted from each other. All this extra shit, this friendly fruit truck revamp shit, it's unnecessary."

I couldn't even look at him while I was saying it because my heart knew that none of it was true.

"Is that how you feel?" He asked. The sorrow in his voice was evident even without seeing it on his face.

"It is." I replied, turning back around to face him. "I'm not one of those girls you can impress with nostalgia and big powder blue rooms that your grandmother probably wants to fill with a grandson. It's sweet, but..."

"Then what can I do?" He threw his hands out to the side. "And for the record, I'm not the typa dude who has to ask that question."

"Yet here you are." I shook my head.

"You could use an attitude adjustment. You know that? All I've been is kind to you and you act like you don't appreciate it."

"Appreciate it? Are you fucking serious?" I snapped, stepping right up in his face, so close that if I blinked, my lashes would've brush his nose.

"I'm pretty sure we've already gone over this, but we fucked. Okay? We had consensual sex. And it wasn't my intention for you to wake up the next morning whipped, but apparently that's exactly what happened. Now you can mope around, searching for ways to change the girl who only wanted to *fuck* you into the girl who wants to bear your first-born son, but that's not gonna change the fact that I don't want you like that."

"Just me or anybody?" He asked, voice even and unfazed by my little rant. "And feel free to be honest." He breathed out, breath hitting my nose like a warm cloud of masculinity.

And I couldn't answer him. Not with the lump that had lodged itself in my throat, making it impossible to breathe easily, let alone speak. A wave came over me that I couldn't escape. I was about to be full on crying in this man's house and my emotions would not be tamed.

"I'm sorry." I said, trying and failing to stop my lips from trembling. "I need... I'm gonna go lay down. Excuse me." I brushed past him, storming in the direction that we'd come from.

"Jo!" He yelled after me. "Jo, come on. I'm sorry!" I could hear him gaining on me.

"Jo, stop, man!" He was right behind me, one hand planted on the base of my hip as he smashed into my back.

"I'm sorry." He pulled my behind against him, leaning down to whisper in my ear from behind. "Whatever I said wrong, I take it back, alright?" His breath was so soothing against my neck, I would've given anything to feel that all over me.

But I didn't know how to ask for it. I couldn't figure out what to say.

"You wanna talk about it?" Skoby's body was still pressed against mine, and I was surprised that I didn't feel his erection forming yet.

"I can't have you in here crying, Jo. Just tell me what's wrong."

"I don't have to tell you anything." I stayed within his embrace, finding comfort in it.

"Then don't." He wrapped both arms around my waist and squeezed me tight, kissing my neck and setting my insides on fire.

"But I want to." I whimpered, moisture pooling between my

legs.

"Then *do*." He whispered in my ear again before slipping the robe off of my shoulder and trailing kisses down the side of my neck until he reached the bend it my shoulder.

We were out in the open, literally in the middle of the hallway, and he was kissing me like we'd made it back into his bedroom. My chest heaved, knees weak and nearly trembling. I reached both arms up and back, around the back of his neck to hold his head in place. I'd done all the resisting I was gonna do that night.

"Let's go back to your room." I purred in his ear.

"I won't make it that far!" He spun me around and hoisted me up of the floor. My legs wrapped around his waist almost involuntarily. Skoby's lips pressed against mine, tongue slipping into my mouth and painting the inside. He tasted just like I'd remembered; smooth and addicting.

Steps rushed by the need to have me naked, he hurried us back down the hallway and into the empty, powder blue room. I'd never fucked on a bare floor before. But with him, I couldn't imagine any place not being an option. As he slammed the door behind us, reaching back with one hand to secure the lock while the other stayed wrapped snug around my waist, I ripped my T shirt up and off over my head, exposing my hard nipples to the chill of the empty room. Without hesitance, Skoby took my nipples into his mouth one by one, sucking them so hard it made my chest cave, dick throbbing against the thin fabric of my panties.

And I was wet.

So wet that it was almost embarrassing. I'd been wanting this mother fucker since the last time I'd had him, and if I wasn't gonna admit it, my pussy sure as hell was.

Dragging his teeth down my nipples, leaving a sting that didn't hurt bad enough for me to want him to stop, he raised his head and stared at me, a stare that scared me because I felt it more than he probably knew. In an attempt to break that stare before I started crying like an idiot, I tilted back and grabbed the hem of his shirt, rolling it up his abs and peeling it off over his head. He was so beautiful, perfect even. And I'd promised myself that I wouldn't do this to myself again when I fled from his home that morning. Yet here I was, heart pumping against his chest as he pulled me in and took my lips into his mouth.

Skoby's big hands were gripping my ass so tight, I could damn near feel his finger prints. I grinded against him, feeling his satin basketball shorts against the back of my thighs, legs wrapped tight around his waist while his dick rose between my legs. Without needing instructions, I loosened my thighs and reached down in the space between us, working my thumbs under the waistband of his shorts and pushing them down around his thighs. Under less heated circumstances, I would've called him out for not having on any underwear. But I was too busy gripping his hard dick in my hand to give a fuck. Boxers were just one less thing blocking me from getting him inside of me. As big as this room was, there was no space for words. The look in Skoby's eyes said that he wanted to ask if I was sure, but the look in mine along with my tongue blazing a trail across my lips, was all the answer he needed to rush me back against the wall, sweep my panties aside with his fingers, and plunge into me so hard that my titties jolted upward. He caught a nipple between those sexy as lips. My eyes fell closed as he sucked it hard, then popped open when he did the same to the other, but harder. Skoby felt like the whole world in my pussy, and my body felt like outer space. Flashes of light sparked in sync with each thrust. I didn't even bother to pacify my screams as he'd assured me that no one would hear us under the rumbling thunder and pouring rain. My ass cheeks smashed against the cool wall, pussy pleasantly swollen, being stretched to capacity by his throbbing cock. I rolled my hips to invite more of him inside me, as if there was space. The sting of his nails digging into my lower back to stop me from escaping was almost more than I could take. I leaned forward to suck his neck—you know, some form of reciprocation for the way he was making me feel. Then he pulled my legs from around his waist, and slid me down until my bare feet were touching the cool floor.

I looked up at him curiously without an audible question on my tongue. I could only imagine what else he was gonna do to me, lowering his shorts and stepping out of them, dick standing at full attention and ready to wreak havoc on my body with my full fucking permission. The tall, dark, and dangerously handsome man that I'd sworn to pry my thoughts away from, was now down on his knees, staring straight up into my eyes before turning me around, bending me at the waist, spreading my ass cheeks apart, and slipping a single digit inside my pussy while I braced my palms against the wall and looked back and down at him with the desperate need to cum written all over my face.

I faced the wall and purred because it was the only way to breathe as his warm tongue bathed my pussy lips. My back caved as he gripped me at the waist, daring me to take my pussy from his hungry mouth for even a second. I spread my legs further apart with influence from his forceful hand, completely exposing myself to him, giving him a full view of what he was tasting, thighs trembling every time his tongue flicked against my clit. He lapped my slick folds with his tongue over and over, periodically suckling at my clit until it felt like it was on fire. He wet his thumb with juices from my creaming pussy then slid it inside my asshole, pulling a moan from my lips that I didn't even recognize.

"Fuuck!" I couldn't help it. I'd never been fucked in the ass by anything, and didn't expect it to feel so good.

Taking cues from my body, he kept his thumb there inside me while he continued to lick my pussy vigorously.

"You like that?" He pulled his tongue from my split for a second. "Tell me you like it." I looked down to find his eyes on me.

I couldn't speak, too locked up in pleasure to say a word. So I nodded and he shoved his thumb further up my ass.

With my palms still planted against the cold wall, I bent over further to give Skoby more access while I took over fingering my pussy.

Then "Nah uh." He pulled my fingers from my pussy and stood up, standing me straight up and pushing the front of me against the wall with his chest pressed against my back. "I don't want nothin in that pussy but me." He leaned down and turned my head, squeezing my cheeks while he sucked my tongue out of my mouth.

"You hear me, Jo?" He slid away from my tongue to ask, to which I desperately nodded *yes* before he was sucking my tongue again.

Skoby pushed his knee between my legs and swept my thighs apart, squatted low enough to anchor himself inside my, then literally stood up in my pussy. I saw so many fucking colors when I closed my eyes. Breasts smashed against the wall as he buried himself inside me. He breathed hard against my neck, moaning profanities about how good, and warm and tight my pussy felt. I rolled with his thrust as hard as I could, throwing my ass back against his pelvis. He sucked away at the sensitive skin on my neck, then stepped back to bend me at the waist, holding me steady as he shoved inside of and pounded away at me like he knew I needed it. Then there was that thumb sliding into my ass again, wet with spit that he'd dropped from his mouth. I had no idea anal play could be so pleasurable. I'd only related that typa shit to pain. But it was blissful having two holes filled simultaneously. He could've done that nasty shit to me all night with no objection.

"Got damn!" He moaned from behind me, the sound of his voice alone damn near drove me over the edge. "Pussy so mother fuckin' good, Jo!"

Skoby was fucking me like he owned me. Didn't ask me for shit. Just took what he wanted and gave what I needed. My hair was swinging wildly over my face, blood rushing to my head due to the fact that he had bent me all the way over, and had me gripping my ankles for balance because the wall seemed to be taking away from the power of his stroke. A heat pooled at my core that was takin everything not to succumb to, breasts swinging beneath me like two ripe melons, turning me on in ways I didn't think possible. I could hardly breathe, and honestly didn't care.

With his pelvis slamming into my ass, thumb probing my asshole, dick deep in my pussy, sweat dripping down his chest and cascading down over me, all I wanted was to feel him painting the walls of my pussy with cum, and to cover his dick with mine.

The harder he pumped into me the dizzier I got, until I could no longer hold it in, and I came in what had to be the most awkwardly pleasing position there was to cum in. With my bottom lip pulled between my teeth, I rocked back against Skoby, giving him all I had left. The relief of feeling that warm fluid spilling out inside me then flowing down the inside of my thighs was like crossing the finish line at the end of a marathon. I was so fucking thirsty, but too immersed in bliss to ask for a drink.

"Where you goin?" I asked, after he'd lowered us both to the floor, then got up to slip his shorts back on.

"Water, towels, and a blanket." He looked back at me and smiled before twisting the door open. "And maybe a snack, cause we ain't finished!"

Skoby

I'd completely lost what was left of my mind between rounds two and three. Sexing this woman on top of a comforter from the linen closet, knowing damn well it wasn't good for either of our backs or knees. I was numb, to be honest. Didn't give a damn about how sore I'd be the next morning. She'd finally allowed me to have her again, and I wasn't about to complain about where.

Lying there on the floor with a pillow under my head and her head on my chest, fingers massaging her scalp through a full head of hair that smelled like vanilla beans and some other shit that I couldn't put my finger on, I felt more at ease than I'd ever remembered feeling. Jo was relaxing to me. Once she dropped her guard, she was fucking perfect. But with the highs of climax wearing off, I knew that little smart mouth wouldn't stay shut for long.

"We can't lay here all night, you know?" She whispered, warm breath rolling over my nipple, head nestled against my chest, contradicting the words coming out of her mouth.

"Why not?" I grumbled. I'd fallen asleep after that last round and neither of us had spoken since.

"Krissi? Gams? I don't want them seeing me walking outta here looking well-fucked and exhausted." She still hadn't lifted her head from my chest, and I wasn't gonna ask her to.

"What time is it anyway?" She asked.

"It was eleven when I left for the last round of water and snacks. So, I don't know, bout one." I'd left my phone in the room. Noticing how aware she was of her surroundings made me wanna block out as many distractions as I could. "Why, you got somewhere you need to be?"

"Yes. Back in the guest room where your grandmother and daughter think I'm sleeping." She lifted her head from my chest, hair smashed on one side, but still so damn pretty. "Come on, get up." She pressed a hand to my chest, and even that made me wanna lay there longer.

"What if I don't want to?" I looked up at her, reaching up to stroke a hand down the side of her face. "Just thirty more minutes." I begged with my eyes. Not a woman alive could say no to my eyes.

"*Fine!*" She said, pushing my hand away and dropping her head back on my chest. "But this'll be a lazy fuck, cause my legs are noodles at this point." I could feel her cheeks fluffing into a smile against my chest.

"Who said anything about fucking, pervert?" I jokingly pushed her head to the side.

"Really, Skoby?" She looked up at me, grinning.

"Yes, really, Jole—Jo." I caught myself about to make the mistake of calling her by her name again. "I'm not tryna kill you *or* myself on this hard ass floor."

She busted out laughing. One of the most annoying, high pitched noises I'd ever heard. But it could easily top my top three favorite because when Jo laughed, you knew it wasn't faked.

"That's funny?" I poked her side, making her laugh even harder.

"It is. And stop!" She swatted my hand. "Lemme find out you fake fit."

"Fake fit? The hell is that?" I adjusted the pillow under my head and looked down at her face, admiring that easy smile and the way she was so comfortable naked around me.

"It's when you amp up your sex game to make it look like you're in shape, then complain about fucking on hardwood floors and such. Were you putting on for me, Skoby? You ain't gotta lie to kick it!" She twisted my nipple between her fingertips, sexy lips spreading into a seductive smile that had my dick jumping under the cover.

"I ain't never faked shit in my whole life, lil mama. And I ain't about to start now." I breathed out and pulled her in closer by the waist, basking in this moment before it slipped away.

"Whatever." She rolled her eyes and laid her head back down. Despite her protests, she didn't wanna leave this room any more than I did. "What are we supposed to do for the next twenty minutes?"

"I said thirty." I reminded her.

"And you used about ten tryna convince me that you ain't fake fit."

"Bet. Make a suggestion and I'm rolling with it." I said, staring up at the ceiling, because if I looked down at that face too long, I'd have her on top of me, doing what she said she didn't wanna do.

"Cool. Twenty-one questions divided by seven."

"So, three questions?" I smirked.

"That takes care of one of my questions." She giggled. "You can at least perform simple math."

"You know you got a smart mouth for somebody laying naked on a comforter in an empty room." I joked.

"And you're pretty judgmental for a nigga lying next to me, *just* as naked, in the same damn room!" She snapped, head up, eyes on me, cracking a smile before laughing out loud. "I'll go first." She dug her elbow into my outstretched forearm and rested her head on her knuckles.

"Bet." I grunted, placing a hand under my head for elevation.

"Your name, where'd it come from?" I'd been asked that question a million times, but only answered it once for my boy Smitty.

"Damn. Straight to the hard shit, huh?" I threw my head back and took a deep breath.

"If it makes you uncomfortable—"

"Nah, I'mma answer." I cut her off. "Cause I don't want you using that lame excuse when it's my turn to ask the questions."

"Fair enough." She shrugged her shoulders.

"Skoby's my biological father's last name." I said just as easily as I'd give somebody the name of my first car. "He was married. My mama was a young jump off, and she couldn't give me his last name without stirring up some shit. So, she made it my first name and that was that."

"Damn. Was he in your life at all?" She asked, eyes squinting with sincerity.

"You know that's a second question, right?" I glanced down at her.

"Yes. Now answer it."

"No. Never met the dude." I replied quickly and honestly. "Next question."

"Ok." She sat up and crossed her legs, titties sitting so pretty I wanted to swallow them up, pussy lips still visibly swollen from me fucking her way too hard. "Why did Gams raise you?" Her shoulders slumped, sending her breasts bouncing.

"What makes you think she did?" I took my eyes off her beading nipples to look into her sexy brown eyes.

"Some things you just know." She replied.

"I'd rather not talk about that." I draped a hand across my abs.

"But you said—"

"I'd rather show you." I pulled her arm from across her chest. "Tomorrow. If you don't burn off before I wake up!"

That seemed to be good enough since she didn't pull her hand away. And I said a silent prayer that she'd still be under my roof when the sun rose.

"I think it's my turn now." I grinned, kissing her hand before releasing it. "I'm assuming your pop's name was Joseph based on your name." I started.

"Framing that as a *statement* doesn't make it any less of a *question*. And the answer is yes!" She smiled. "Next question." She rolled her eyes, and I'll be damned if that didn't make me wanna take her down again.

"Why do you call your grandma Mama?" I'd been curious about that. Figured it was the same reason I called mine Gams, but

I couldn't be sure about shit with Jo. She was a fucking Rubik's Cube.

"Cause that's who she is. One question left. Make it count!" She clapped her hands together, making her titties jiggle again. She had no idea how much it turned me on that she didn't give a damn about being so exposed.

"Aight." I had to sit up straight for this one. Couldn't have her looking away or tryna dodge the question like she'd done before. "Who's the only person that can call you by your real name?"

I observed a shift in her demeanor that made me regret asking as soon as the words left my lips. But I wanted to know. If there was anybody out there that was a threat to me being with her, I needed to know who he was and how to make her forget about him. I'd had my past. Was still dealing with it on a daily basis because of Krissi. But I wouldn't let that stop me from pursuing Jo. I was falling for this girl, and as strange is it seemed, I didn't mind.

"Why? Of all the things to wanna know, why do you wanna know that?" She asked. She was redirecting again and that was only making the shit worse.

"Cause I wanna know." I replied.

"But why?"

"Cause I'm feeling you, alright? In case that ain't clear already."

"And what, you wanna know if I'm spoken for? If yours is the only dick I'm riding?"

She was hot, but still sitting. And that was a good sign.

"Yeah. All that." I tipped my chin up. "You got a problem with that?"

She didn't answer fast enough.

"Cause if you do—"

"It's my daddy, okay!?" She cut me off. "And I'm pretty sure thirty minutes is up by now, so can we go?" She stood up and gathered the T shirt and panties she'd abandoned for me hours ago. But I didn't move. Just lay there watching her every move like the pretty ass picture she was.

"Hello? Are you just gonna lay there?" She tilted her head to the side, arms folded across her chest with her weight resting on one perfectly rounded hip.

"Can you come back down here?" I asked, sitting up and spreading my legs out in front of me, open just wide enough for her to sit between them.

"Skoby—"

"I'm not tryna do what you think I'm tryna do." I said, gaining her trust that quickly with the truth in my eyes.

She padded over to me, toenails painted a dark crimson color that would be marked in my mind forever as *Joletta Red*. I knew that unlike most of my past conquest, it would take more than good dick and some money to win this woman over. And that was a good thing because I saw more in her and wanted more from her than a few rolls in the sack could satisfy. The fact that she held so much in meant that she had that much more to offer, and would hopefully come to realize that we were more alike than different. In the brief moment that it took her to lower herself to the floor in front of me, securing her thick, chocolate legs around my waist, pressing herself against me and allowing me to hold her close and kiss her lips, I knew everything I needed to know about her for the time being. That she trusted me enough to open up just a little bit more, and if I played my cards right, I could slowly pry that door open until there was nothing left to hide.

Seven

Skoby

I knew it was too good to be true. My eager ass had pushed too hard and now she'd run off. Looking at the empty bed in my guest room, my heart sank in my chest. I was simping harder than a mother fucker, and this chick wasn't even mine to lose.

I flipped the light off and pulled the door closed. The smell of bacon caught my attention and I knew that Gams and Krissi must've been up early cooking breakfast. When I made it to the bottom of the stairs, I could hear them laughing and talking. But there was a third laugh that I wasn't used to hearing in the mix, and it was too high pitched to belong to Uncle Lem.

Dragging my feet, cause I was tired as shit, I turned the corner into the kitchen on a yawn and a stretch. I'd fixed my mouth to give Gams and Krissi a hard time but was pleasantly surprised to find Jo in the kitchen with them, helping Krissi scoop a pancake off the griddle.

"Good morning, Sunshine!" Gams chirped, forking bacon from a long pan onto a serving dish covered in napkins. "Looks like somebody didn't get much sleep last night." She cut her eyes at me. "Pour you some orange juice." She pointed to the round, glass pitcher filled to the brim with fresh-squeezed juice from an orange tree in the back yard.

"I slept fine, Gams." I shook my head, grabbing the pitcher and filling a tall glass with juice. "Mornin' ladies." I turned my eyes to my little girl and the woman who was responsible for the ache in my back and the bags under my eyes, wondering how she managed to look so damn refreshed.

"Good morning!" Jo winked at me while Gams had turned away to grab a stack of plates from the cabinet.

Slick mother fucker.

"Good morning, Daddy!" Krissi squeaked wearing her favorite pink, silk pajamas, hair wild and all over her head just how she liked it. "Jo showed me how to make animal pancakes. Guess what this one is!?"

She pointed to a pancake that consisted of two small circles and one big one that were all connected. "Ummm, lemme see." I squinted, knowing I wouldn't get the shit right. "That has to be Mickey Mouse." I gave my best guess.

Jo covered her mouth and turned away to laugh.

"Daddy, no!" Krissi folded her arms across her tiny chest, face scrunched with disappointment. "It's a koala bear. See?" She pointed at the pancake harder as if that would make identifying it any easier.

"You know what, that's what I was gonna say at first." I lied through my teeth. "Can you make Daddy one?" I asked to soften the blow of pancake disappointment.

"I guess." She shrugged her shoulders. "Can you help me again, Jo?" She looked up beside her at Jo, who was surprisingly wearing one of Gams's many aprons. Gams never let anybody near her aprons.

"You know what, I got a better idea." I mischievous glimmer took over Jo's eyes that I wasn't comfortable with. "Why don't we let Daddy try it out?" She cut her eyes at me, and I knew right then and there I'd been set up for failure.

"Lord, let me go get this mop!" Gams sighed, heading toward the Butler's closet that the butler never used because we didn't have a butler.

"You gone play me like that, Gams?" I chuckled, rounding the kitchen counter and reaching underneath to grab one of Gams's aprons.

"Bee, the last time I turned you loose in this kitchen we had to repaint the walls." She smirked. "Remember that, Krissi?" She had to pull my baby girl into the mess.

"Yes ma'am!" Krissi giggled. "Daddy got tomato sauce on the light bulbs!" She could hardly gain her composure remembering the one time we made homemade pizza together. That happened a year prior, and needless to say, I hadn't cooked another meal since.

"The sauce was good, though." I defended, securing the apron around my waist after folding down the top half, cause it wouldn't accommodate my chest.

"Yeah, what was left of it!" Gams laughed, returning to the kitchen with a mop and a bucket. "Go head. I'm getting this water ready." She retrieved a bottle of Fabuloso from under the kitchen sink and poured some into the bucket while the tap water ran.

"That's messed up." I slanted my eyes at Gams before bringing them back to Jo who was barely catching her breath from laughing. "You ready, man?" I asked her, poking Krissi in the side while she continued laughing.

"I'on't know. Gams, you got another mop?" She joked, and that was just the kinda shit Gams was down with, throwing her head back, laughing while she filled the bucket with hot water.

Knowing Gams as well as I did, I knew she'd planned on

sweeping and mopping the kitchen whether a mess was made or not. The woman couldn't function if any part of the roof she was under didn't smell like some kind of cleaning solution. And even though she didn't live with me on a permanent basis, while she was there, she treated my house like her home.

Once the three comedians had calmed down enough for me to get to the large bowl of pancake batter, I poured two small circles and one big one onto the griddle under Krissi's watchful eye. She clapped when she noticed how on point my pouring skills were, and Jo gave a hesitant nod, tryna steal my shine. By the time I flipped my koala bear head over, I had em all standing around me on hush mode, picking their faces up off the floor.

"There. Now where's my butter?!" I asked, basking in the opportunity to talk shit, knowing full well I'd prayed through the whole process, cause I was trash in the cooking department.

"Boy, if you don't get that crooked-eared koala and take it to the table!" Gams dismissed me with a flipping hand and a chuckle. "And Krissi, go get Uncle Lem." She said, damn near shocking the socks off my feet.

"Really?" I said, making my way to the dining room behind Jo. "See if Uncle Lem got a thermometer in there, Krissi. I think Gams might have a fever!" I joked, taking in the view of Jo's ass swaying in front of me.

"I heard that!" Gams slanted her eyes at me, placing a big bowl of grits and a tray of scrambled eggs at the center of the table as Jo and I took her seats.

She went off to the kitchen to grab the rest of the feast, leaving me and Jo sitting there alone, which was never a good idea.

"You got something to do with this?" I leaned to the side and asked, placing my hand on the soft skin of her thigh under the table.

"No." She said, squeezing my hand then removing it from her thigh, placing it on mine, and giving it another squeeze, I guess to let me know she wasn't tripping. "She must've had a change of heart or something. People do that, ya know?" She winked at me.

"Yeah. Gams ain't *people* though." I sighed, all fucked up by whatever was going on.

"You can sit by me, Uncle Lemon!" Krissi's voice came singing into the dining room, holding onto Uncle Lem's hand like he was the three-foot tall four-year-old, and she was the six-foot tall sixty-year-old, mispronouncing his name even after we'd told her his name was Lemont. "We made koala pancakes. Jo showed me how to do it on the grizzle!"

"It's a griddle, Krissi." I corrected. "Good morning, Unc." I nodded at Uncle Lem as he took his seat under the supervision of little Miss Boss Lady.

"Good morning." He nodded at me and Jo, a gentle smile crossing his slim face. Rumor has it Uncle Lem was a lady killer back in the day, and I'm sure it had a lot to do with those heavy lidded ass eyes. "Julia must be tryna poison me!" He joked. "I ain't sat at this table since she had it moved in."

"Ain't nobody tryna kill you, Lemont!" Gams reentered the dining room carrying a pitcher of orange juice and a fresh pot of coffee for her and Uncle Lem. "If that was the case I coulda took you out a long time ago. Now hush and drink this coffee. I made it cowboy strength."

She carefully filled his favorite cup to the brim when he extended it in her direction, shaking his head the whole time. Those two had a love-hate relationship that had been playing out for as long as I could remember. A slight rift grew between them when Gramps passed away. I didn't know why and wasn't sure how to ask. All I knew was that they loved each other like sisters and brothers, and even if they didn't eat meals in the same room or sit and talk regularly, that love was always there in the subtlest ways. Krissi was as pleased as punch to have Uncle Lem sitting at the table with everybody. She'd been running off to eat with him in the media room since I bought the house, and I never considered the fact that she might be feeling torn about having to do that all the time. Whatever the case, I didn't think she'd have to do it anymore. Gams seemed to be turning a corner with her tolerance of Uncle Lem smacking like a cow. She even turned on some soft jazz on the P.A. system that ran throughout the house to help drown it out. Best compromise I'd seen that woman make in a long time.

"Everybody good? We got enough left for seconds." Gams stood from the table, prepared to take everybody's empty plates.

"I'm good, Gams." I rubbed my belly.

"Me too." Krissi leaned back in her seat with her belly poking out.

"Everything was delicious." Jo pushed away from the table then stood up to help clear the plates.

"I'm full as a tick." Uncle Lem patted his stomach then pushed back from the table too.

"Lemont, if you don't mind, I'd like to talk to you once I get these dishes cleaned." Gams eyes went across the table to Uncle Lem before he could stand.

"Gams, we can get the dishes." I stood up, gathered the rest of the plates and took off behind Jo toward the kitchen. "Krissi, go wash your hands and grab your Kindle." I instructed. "I downloaded some new books for you last week."

"Yes!" She pulled a balled fist in beside her waist, hopping out of her seat and rushing down the hallway to wash her hands.

While Jo and I busied ourselves with the dishes, Gams took a seat at the table beside Uncle Lem. We were both quiet, bending our ears to hear as much as we could. Imagine my surprise when Gams came right out and apologized to Uncle Lem for making him feel like he wasn't welcome at the dinner table all those times.

By the time it was all over, they'd gotten up and hugged. I

hadn't seen them do that since the last day Gramps was alive. The whole dynamic of the relationship confused me sometimes. Their sole connection had been her husband—his brother. And now that he was gone, shit had to be awkward to navigate through.

In any event, they were at peace. And that was more than I could ask for, and definitely more than I'd expected. With the kitchen pre-cleaned and Krissi tucked away in a nook full of pillows that Gams had created for her in a cozy corner of the living room, it was time to take Jo home after making a quick trip down memory lane.

Jo

"Where's Uncle Lem?" I asked when Skoby came into the living room jingling a set of keys.

"He's off today. I'm driving." He said. "You ready?"

"Wait, you can drive?" I teased, standing from his chocolate brown leather sofa and grabbing my purse.

"Funny." He dipped his chin, punching a code into the alarm system. "I already shut y'all up in the kitchen. You tryna make this two and O for ya boy?"

"Whatever!" I brushed past him as he held the tall door open. "Even a broken clock is right twice a day. You just make sure you get me home in one piece." I switched on out to the wide front porch, peeping over my shoulder and catching him taking a look at my ass. The poor man couldn't help himself.

Amongst a neighborhood filled with older modeled homes, this negro managed to navigate his way to an empty lot. With the empty room in his house and now this empty spot of land, I was starting to think maybe Skoby thought I liked nothingness. He'd told me before we left his house that he needed to stop somewhere before he took me home, and in my mind, I'd assumed it was a drug run or something since that's what I'd assumed he did for money before discovering he'd actually inherited his grandfather's produce business. All the tattoos and just his demeanor would lead anybody to believe he was a dope boy. Guess that's what I get for judging books by their covers. Skoby was no more into drug trafficking than my scary ass.

"Come on." He pulled up alongside the empty lot that had caught my attention amongst the many homes that lined a street that was riddled with potholes, and hopped out.

"Are you about to kill me or something?" I asked as he pulled my door open and extended a hand to help me out of the old powder blue Chevy truck he'd driven us over in.

The smell of it reminded me of the days when my grandpa was alive and would take me and Mama fishing at the Texas City dike. The smell of the exhaust from his tailpipe paled in comparison to all the toxins we smelled driving through Texas City. But it was worth the funk to come home with a cooler full of catfish that Mama would be scaling and frying the next day.

"In broad daylight? Come on, Jo. I'd at least wait til it's dark out." He winked, holding onto my hand as he led me toward the empty lot.

"You ain't funny." I pinched him at the waist.

"And you're paranoid." He looked down to the side at me. "We're here to answer one of your questions from last night, about my mama." He came to a stop at the sidewalk.

Down the length of the road, the grass in every yard was neatly trimmed, a direct contrast to the bumpy roads that were more than likely the result of negligent city officials. And the lot in front of us was no different. The lawn had been kept as if someone was still living there. Granted, there wasn't a home or even so

101

much as a tree in the yard, there was definitely an owner who cared about this space very much.

"Did she live here?" I asked, watching his dark eyes canvas the area the way one canvas a headstone.

"*We* lived here." He said. "Just me and her." He continued, standing completely still, never taking his eyes off the lot.

With curiosity getting the better of me, I attempted to take a step forward. But I was stopped when Skoby gripped my hand tighter and held me in place beside him.

"I just wanted you to see it." He said. "You ready to go home?" He asked.

"I... yeah." I looked up at him, trying my best to decipher what he might be thinking and coming up with nothing.

"You okay?" I asked with his hand still clinching mine tight.

"Yeah. I'm good." He pulled his eyes away from the lot to look at me. "I'm good." He brought my hand to his soft lips and kissed it, then turned us around and walked back to the truck.

My place was only a short distance away and that was fortunate because Skoby wasn't talking much. In the short time that we'd spent together, I'd gotten so used to being the quiet one, the one so distracted by my problems that I couldn't open up to the possibility of anything good, that I never considered maybe he was dealing with shit too.

But he was.

It was written all over his face. Something about that lot where he and his mother used to live had flipped a switch in his spirit, and I didn't like what it was bringing about. I was just starting to find reasons to like the dude, and maybe not be so adamant about pushing him away. And now he wants to give me reason to doubt my instincts? He should've shown me this side before I fell asleep in his arms in an empty ass room.

We pulled up alongside Mama's and he turned off the ignition. The silence didn't seem so loud with the old Chevy running. But now that the roar was gone, the silence was filling up actual space.

"Skoby, if you wanna talk about it—"

"I don't." He cut me off, eyes scrunched under thick brows, lips balled up as if they were holding back words he didn't wanna speak. "I'm good, aight? I'mma hit you up later."

"Okay." I said, reaching across the cracking leather seat to grip his hand, staring into his eyes and finding something there that I was all too familiar with.

"For the record, we have more in common than you know." I said because I felt it in his sweaty palm that that was exactly what he needed to hear.

"Run on up to that door so I can watch that ass jiggle!" He cracked a smile to soften the mood. I popped his hand and climbed out of the truck, running up to the door as he'd requested, so he could watch my sore ass jiggle.

Eight

Skoby

It had been a long day for me and Mama. She'd worked a double shift at one of Gramps's produce factories, when one of the line workers didn't show up. Mama was a lead supervisor and didn't ever have to get her hands dirty. Didn't even have to work, as far as my grandfather was concerned. But she was determined to earn her keep and not live off her father's money.

She'd picked me up from Gams and Gramps a little later than usual and offered to stop by McDonald's to grab something quick to eat since she wouldn't have time to cook dinner. But I insisted on a bowl of Spaghetti-O's, because everything tasted better when prepared by Mama's hands. We made it to our house about fifteen minutes later. I hurried through my bath while Mama straightened the living room. When I'd finished getting dressed, she poured the Spaghetti-O's in a pot, then turned on the stove and went into the bathroom to run her bath water. It seemed like only a few minutes had passed between the time Mama went into the bathroom and the time I'd sat down in front of the TV in my room. But apparently, it had been much longer, because when I got up during a commercial break to check on a burning smell and to see why Mama hadn't yelled down the hall to tell me my food was ready, the hallway was filled with smoke. The bathroom that Mama was in was on the other side of the house, and the way things were situated, I'd have to pass through the kitchen to get to her. But I couldn't. There was so much smoke in the air I couldn't even see the kitchen, much less pass through it. And due to the fact that our faulty smoke-detector hadn't made a sound, I needed to get to the other side of the house through a side window that led into Mama's bedroom, and let her know that she needed to get out.

Having left my shoes at the front door like I always did because Mama didn't want me tracking dirt on her light brown carpet, I slipped them on and ran out of the door to go knock on the window and tell Mama to climb out. It was too high up for me to hop in, but just high enough for my knuckles to reach. Mama's bathroom and bedroom were connected, so she'd surely be able to hear me.

After what seemed like an eternity of knocking on the window without any response from Mama, our neighbor, Mrs. Blue, from across the street, ran up and asked if I was okay. I gave her the run down, stuttering and crying and trying to tell her that my mama was inside the burning house. She grabbed me by the hand and ran me across the street to her house. Flames were shooting from the roof, a large portion of them from right over Mama's bedroom.

While sitting on Mrs. Blue's couch, I heard sirens blaring down our street. She wouldn't let me look out of the window and assured me that everything would be alright. And I believed her because I was six and she was an adult, and adults didn't lie to children.

But she had.

She'd stood right in my face, handing me cookies and milk and a warm blanket to wrap myself in, and lied to me right up to the minute that Gramps and Gams came to pick me up from her house.

It took years for me to stop sitting on my grandparents' porch every day, waiting for Mama to come back from wherever she'd gone. I understood that death was final. Gramps had explained it to me the best he knew how. But there was something about not being able to see her lying in a coffin that wouldn't let the thought of her being dead settle in my mind. I learned later that they'd found her in the kitchen, more than likely trying to get to me. Her body was so badly burned that a closed casket funeral was the only option. Seemed like the whole thing was a dream that I'd wake up from and find her standing there. I knew it wouldn't make sense to anybody else, so I kept it to myself and hadn't shared it with anyone to this day. But I blamed myself for Mama's death for a long time. If I'd only settled for a Happy Meal, she would still be here with me.

I wanted to tell Jo all of this while we stood in front of the property where Mama had taken her last breath. I'd actually planned on it. But when the moment came, I realized that it was too big a feat. And not for Jo. It was too big for me.

Nine

Jo

With Mama at Aunt Janine's, I had time to clean and clear my mind without distractions, and maybe even get some writing in. Though everything in our place except for the bedroom set I'd brought with me when I moved back in, was old and worn, a little *TLC* was all it took to make it sparkle just enough to feel like home. Mama'd taught me a million ways to make old things new. I could remember us finding the dinette table that was sitting in her kitchen, at a thrift store for fifteen dollars. And we found four mismatched chairs for a dollar a piece that same day, to go around it. And they were perfect, because each of them seemed to have their own personality.

My favorite, and the one I plopped down in at every meal, had been the pink one that sat on the side of the table closest to the dining room wall. Mama's was a deep blue one with a cushioned seat at one end of the table, and Grand Daddy's was a pale gray one with blonde wood armrests that sat at the head of the table. I swear, all three of those chairs looked so much like us that when I looked at em, even when they were empty, it seemed like they were looking back at me. The fourth one was fire engine red, and only got sat in on the rare occasion that my biological mother stopped by. But she wouldn't be sitting in it again any time soon. Actually, never would be fine with me.

Running a feather duster over the red seat and the gray one was almost enough to take my mind on a trip down a tunnel that never had light at the end. And I wasn't tryna do that. Not with the scent of bleach filling up Mama's old house. This was a time for cleaning, not crying.

I quickly left the dining room after I was satisfied with what I'd done and went on to sweeping before I finally got to my favorite cleaning task, mopping. It meant that every other level had been wiped clean and there was nothing left but the floor. About two rounds of clean, soapy and bleachy mop water was all it took to cover the small, three-bedroom home, and I was done with my chores all within three hours.

It surprised me that Aunt Janine hadn't called or come by to drop Mama off. And as soon as I decided it was okay to pull out my lap top and type out a few words, my phone vibrated against the coffee table and sent me spiraling back into reality.

"Jo, you at the house?" Aunt Janine's voice sounded hurried and out of breath.

"Yeah. Is everything okay? Mama alright?" I asked with hesitance, because I'd heard hurried and out of breath voices before, and that never meant good news.

"I'm coming to get you." She said without answering my question.

"Aunt Janine, is something wrong with Mama?" I asked again. "Just tell me!" I couldn't compose myself.

"Jo, just… I'll be there in ten minutes, okay?" She said before hanging up. And I could hear the lump in her throat through the damn phone.

9

I wanted to talk to him. Not my best friend who'd been blowing up my phone since she somehow got the news that Mama'd had a heart attack, or my aunt who was sitting next to me bawling in the waiting room of the same negligent ass hospital that my grandfather had died in all those years ago.

But him.

Because I'd seen in his eyes that he knew how it felt to lose the person who meant the world to you. And he'd be the only one to understand how I was feeling right now.

"I'm going outside for some fresh air." I stood from the cold, hard, plastic chair that was reminding me that I had skin, because at the moment, it didn't feel like I did.

I'd gone in and kissed Mama's forehead, hoping that maybe her eyes would pop open and she'd tell me that this was all a bad dream, and everything would be okay. I'd just cleaned her house from top to bottom, for God's sake. The least she could do was wake up and come see it. Aunt Janine didn't say a word as I stood from my chair. Probably couldn't even see me through all the tears in her eyes. The doctor had come out and told us that there was nothing more that they could do. They were waiting on one of us to tell them to pull the plug.

And I couldn't do that.

I *wouldn't* do that.

This woman had dropped everything to provide a safe place for me to live when neither of my parents could. And now I was supposed to just give up and let her go? I hadn't even come close to thanking her for all she'd done for me, and if that plug got pulled I never would. Sure, she knew I loved her. I told her every day. But I just needed more time. Why couldn't I just have more time?

The cool October chill crept up out of nowhere as the doors to the emergency room slid open and I walked through them to get some fresh air in my lungs. Every star in the sky was lit, and they all seemed to be looking down on me, taunting me, because they were tucked away safe up in the sky without having to deal with stupid shit like death. I wished I had a rock and an arm strong enough to throw it up in the air and knock down every damn star. That's the kind of pain I was dealing with. The kind that invades your mind with silly and impossible thoughts.

It couldn't've been any later than seven p.m. but it felt so much later than that. My phone buzzed in my pocket and I pulled it out prepared to ignore Nessa's twentieth call. But when I looked at the screen and saw that it was Skoby, I felt like maybe the stars weren't taunting me after all.

"Jo." He said. And his tone let me know that Nessa had somehow gotten ahold of him.

"I don't know what I'm supposed to do." I replied. I hadn't even cried. Felt like if I started I might never stop.

"You still at the hospital?" He asked, the sound of wind whistling in the background.

"Yeah." I said, flopping down on a concrete bench outside the emergency room doors.

"I'm on my way." He said, and he stayed on the phone for the next twenty minutes, driving and listening to me breathe.

Skoby

I didn't wanna hang up, because as long as I could hear her breathing I knew that she was ok. Or at least alive. Losing somebody that close to you can drive people to dangerous places in their thoughts, and I didn't have to know Jo her whole life to know that her grandmother was the most important person in her life.

"Smitty, I know we gotta get this done, but I can't talk right now, bro." I'd pulled up to the hospital and was on my way to the emergency room entry where I hoped Jo was still waiting.

Me and Smitty had been working on getting some fruit stands set up in under privileged areas in addition to a regular route for the fruit truck, and we were only a week out from the job fair where we'd be hiring roughly thirty new employees to man the stands and drive the trucks. I understood the importance of making and meeting deadlines better than most since I was usually the one on top of shit. But for the first time in a long time, I had to shift my priorities. Jo needed me, and Smitty was fully capable of picking up my slack for a minute. He really didn't have much of a choice.

"Bro, you met this chick five minutes ago." He continued his argument. "I know she fine and shit but—"

"It ain't that. And watch ya mouth." I cut him off before he said something that had me driving to the Woodlands to set his ass straight. "All that's left to do is shoot emails to the other vendors and make sure they got the schedules last week. Did Yoni send you the mailing list?"

"She did. But—"

"Then hit em up." I rushed through the crowded parking lot, pavement slick from rain and a chill in the air from the cold front that had just dropped. "There should be like twenty of em. We can touch base tomorrow."

"Bro, why can't Yomi send this shit? She's your assistant."

"Because if Yoni sends it, it ain't personal. We're tryna be personal, remember? Let the people know we're using our own hands to make shit happen. Listen, I gotta go, Smitt." I breathed into the phone, finally reaching the emergency entrance and spotting Jo sitting on a bench outside the sliding doors.

"Aight, holla." Smitty said before I ended the call and dropped my phone in the side pocket of my jeans.

Had I not been on the phone with this nigga talking in circles for the last ten minutes, I might've had time to think of what to say to a beautiful stranger whose life had just been flipped upside down. With her sitting out front, I couldn't even run to the gift shop to grab a bear, or flowers, or whatever people buy to bring smiles to someone's face when smiling is the last thing they wanna do. Her hair was pulled up into a knot on top of her head, and the ripped blue jeans she was wearing, exposing slits of her smooth chocolate thighs, weren't suitable for fighting the chill outside, nor was the thin tank top that exposed her blooming cleavage. Stride slowed by people rushing to and fro, I got to her as fast as I could, then pulled off my hoodie and kneeled down in front of her.

I tipped her chin up, needing to see those eyes because it felt like too long since the last time I had. "You gotta be freezing." I said.

She nodded her head *yes* and allowed me to slip the hoodie down over her head, holding her arms up and pushing them through the sleeves.

I stood from squatting and took a set beside her, leaning forward and resting my arms on my thighs. I didn't like seeing her like this. Sitting in this kind of silence. But I knew from experience that it was necessary. Sometimes the pain is too much to speak through.

After a minute, or five, or ten, she took a deep breath and looked out at the busy roadway in front of us.

"I don't know what I'm supposed to do." She said, almost whispered. "Her soul is gone but her body's still in there and they're asking me to let that go too."

She sniffed and her eyes glistened, and I thought she might cry. But she didn't. Just kept her eyes fixed on the roadway like the answer to her question was out there.

"What would you do?" She asked, turning her eyes to me.

I swallowed hard, realizing that I was safer in silence now that she was asking me to speak. "I don't know." Was all I could say without my voice cracking. I wished I'd had more but I didn't.

I reached to the side and grabbed ahold of her hand, hoping that was enough to let her know that I was there for her in whatever capacity she needed me. After a few minutes of sitting side by side with our hands being the warmest things on our bodies, Jo's aunt came outside to let her know that it was time to decide what they were gonna do. Overwhelmed by the decision, Jo left it up to her aunt who without a second thought decided to take Mama Jo off life support and move ahead with funeral arrangements.

I sat outside in the waiting room through the process which couldn't've lasted more than thirty minutes. I'd gone through the same with my grandfather and didn't want any parts of standing in that room when the last breath left her body. Jo was already different from any woman I'd ever been with, and I knew that this was only gonna change her more. I didn't question my ability to hold her down, but I couldn't help but wonder if she'd let me.

Ten

Jo

She'd been gone three weeks and I still hadn't cried. Couldn't sleep for more than an hour at a time because everything in the house reminded me of her. The smell of it. All the whatnots sitting on shelves. Old pictures of family members whom I hadn't seen in years before they showed up at her funeral, one being her daughter, my mother, who'd fallen on hard times and only showed up to see if Mama'd left her any money.

And she hadn't. Aside from the house, which was at least five years behind in taxes, Mama didn't leave anything for anybody. It didn't take a full twenty-four hours after Mama's coffin was lowered into the ground before my birth mother boarded a plane and returned to whatever hole she'd climbed out of.

We'd never been close, not even for the six years that we lived together a block down from Mama and Grand Daddy in a run-down apartment complex that had since been demolished. My Mama was a selfish woman, and only used me as a means to keep tabs on my father. But when he was shot to death by her live-in boyfriend after stopping by unannounced to check on me, she no longer had use for me at all. Literally sat me down on Mama's couch one day, and left without so much as a kiss on the forehead.

We both blamed each other for my father's death. She said that if he wasn't so dead-set on stopping by to see me before he went off to work on an oil rig for the next three weeks, he'd've never come in contact with her jealous ass boyfriend and would still be alive to *maybe* make us a family again. That logic made sense when I was six, and it kept me up plenty of nights well into pubescence, even though Mama and Grand Daddy told me it was a stupid lie from the pit of hell. But now, as a grown ass woman, I knew that the woman simply couldn't take responsibility for her actions. She wanted Daddy to be coming over to check on *her*. To beg her to take him back when that had been the last thing on his mind. She didn't think I could remember her standing aside and watching Daddy and that fool nigga, Johnny Lee, tussling at the front door. But I did. Stood there at the end of the hallway crying my eyes out because everything was so loud and all I wanted to do was hug my Daddy and kiss him goodbye. It was all fine and good in her eyes, having two men fighting, one over her and the other, trying to see his baby girl. But that stupid smile fell off her face when Johnny Lee's gun went off, shooting my daddy in the chest and ending his life at the age of twenty-four.

I'd long since, gotten used to living without my daddy, but never got over the way that things were handled. Any attempt made to reach out to my mother always ended in an argument, and I'd given it my last shot five years prior. Mama gave up on tryna make me believe that there was a heart in her daughter's chest that pumped the same blood that flowed through hers and mine. As far as I was concerned, Janice Rene Foster was not my mother. Joletta Rene Foster had taken that title and kept it until the day she died.

Her room sat directly across the hallway from mine, with the door sitting open just like she'd left it. The only thing missing from all the things that reminded me of her was *her*, and that was slowly becoming more than I could take.

"You want me to come over?" Vanessa had been calling me

every hour on the hour. And if it wasn't her blowing up my phone thinking I was suicidal or some shit, it was Skoby offering to bring me food.

But I didn't need food. I'd had more pans of spaghetti than the refrigerator could hold sitting on the curb waiting for the trash man. What I needed was for God to explain why he'd taken away the best thing that ever happened to me and replaced it with emptiness. But that wasn't gonna happen, because if Mama ever taught me anything, it was that you don't question God if you ain't ready for his reply. She always knew what to say to me. How to get my ass in gear. Who was gonna be that person now that she was gone? Who was gonna come along and snap me outta this shit?

Almost as quickly as that question popped into my head, the doorbell rang and I thought it was Vanessa.

"Nessa, I know you ain't pulling a pop-up." I spoke into the receiver. I'd gotten so lost in my thoughts I forgot she was on the phone.

"Girl, I'm on my couch. Go see who it is. Maybe they can drag your stubborn ass outta that house." She smacked her lips.

"Whatever." I sighed. "I'll call you in the morning."

"You mean you'll answer my call in the morning?" She corrected.

"Yeah. That. Bye."

I ended the call and got up off the couch, stretching and yawning because my body was tired, but my mind couldn't rest. Whomever was at the door was about to get turned away. I didn't do pop-ups, especially not with the mood I was in. Or at least that's what I was thinking before I opened the door and saw Skoby standing there wearing a pair of jeans that bent with his bowlegs and a black hoodie that looked a lot like the red one he'd draped over me at the hospital.

"What's that?" I asked looking down at the brown paper bag clutched in his hand.

"*Not* spaghetti." He grinned that grin that always seemed to send my heart racing.

"I'm not hungry, Skoby." I stepped back to let him in out of the cold, the smell of his cologne mixed with what smelled like pepper steak made me change my mind. Suddenly I was starving.

"Why didn't you call?" I asked, walking back over to the couch with him following close behind me after he pulled the door closed.

"I did. Went straight to voicemail." He put the bag down on the coffee table as I flopped down on the couch.

"But you came anyway." I sighed. "How are Gams, Uncle Lem, and Krissi?"

"Are you really asking me that?" He said, looking down at me as he stood in front of me.

"What, I can't ask about them?"

"No. Not when they keep asking about *you* and all I can tell em is that you ain't answering your phone."

"I just talked to you a few days ago." I whined.

"Seven." He corrected. "A solid week. And if it wasn't for work, I woulda been over here sooner. Your hair looks flat. You need to eat." He sat down on the sofa next to me, leaning forward and pulling the contents from the brown paper bag.

"You ain't funny." I pulled my feet under me and crossed my arms.

"But you smiled." He noted, popping open one of two Styrofoam plates. "Pepper steak or T-S-O chicken?"

"It's actually General Tso's chicken." I gave a cringed smile.

"And mix em together."

"My bad, *Chun Lee*." He looked back at me. "And do what?"

I punched the side of his arm. "Mix em!" I laughed a tired laugh. "Sweet and salty is always good." I sat up and grabbed a plastic utensil packet, then forked a piece of beef from one tray and a chunk of chicken from the other.

"Taste it." I put it up to his mouth. "Come on. I promise it's good." He smirked at me, looking down at the fork as I pushed the food up to his lips again until he opened his mouth and hesitantly chomped it off.

"Well?" I asked, waiting for a verdict.

"You know what, it ain't that bad." He said, chewing a mouth full of food.

"Really? I never tried it!" A smile sprung from my cheeks and he knew that he'd been had.

"So, you got games?" He nodded his head while I doubled over laughing. "Real funny." He opened up the other utensils and continued eating.

"My bad." I said, scooting forward on the sofa and digging into the General Tso's chicken. "But that face though!" I covered my mouth laughing again.

"You laughin but that sweet and salty mix might be my new go-to." He mixed another round of chicken and beef and forked it in his mouth.

"You serious ain't you?" I squinted. "Lemme taste it." I asked as he gathered another helping onto his fork.

He guided the food to my mouth, holding my chin like I was a baby trying table-food for the first time. And what my pallet witnessed was nothing short of amazing. We had accidentally stumbled upon something magical all in the name of a gag.

"Dude, this is *fuffing deliffus*!" I spoke through a mouth full of magic before chewing it up and swallowing it down. "This should legit be on the menu."

"I'm tryna tell you." He prepared his next bite. And before we knew it, we'd eaten our way to the bottom of two full plates of food.

While Skoby was up, throwing away our empty plates, Mama's voice sounded in my head for the first time since she'd passed away. She kept telling me to get up, and not in a literal sense. But to get up outta this funk and stop feeling sorry for myself. I'd been staying in the house and avoiding everything outside of it, and in turn, killing my own spirit every day. The lack of sleep and the inability to even mourn her was a direct result of this confined space. I don't know why I didn't realize it before. But it made so much sense when I heard it in her voice.

"Thank you for this." I said to Skoby as he reentered the living room, wiping his hands with a paper towel. "For popping up on me and forcing me to eat, cause honestly I was starving and didn't even realize it until you opened up those plates."

He nodded but didn't say anything because for whatever reason, he always knew what *not* to say.

"I can't stay here." I added as he stood there, seemingly waiting for my next words, so that he could try and fix whatever was wrong, since that was another thing he seemed to be proficient at.

"And please don't offer me a room at your house." I put up a hand, recognizing that look of charity in his woodsy brown eyes.

"Why not?" He asked.

"Because Krissi's there." I replied, standing from the sofa. "Kids are impressionable, and I don't want her thinking I'm a permanent fixture in her life when I'm not."

That statement seemed to affect Skoby in a way he wasn't sure how to respond to. So, he didn't. Instead nodding his head and shoving his hands deep in the pockets of his jeans.

"Cool." He said. "You can crash at my old apartment." He pulled a set of keys from his pockets, slid one off the keyring and handed it to me. "The lease stands til the end of the year. If you need it longer than that, let me know."

He backed away and sat down in the big, worn chair on the opposite side of the tiny living room. I flipped the key around in my hand, completely blown away by the fact that this man could afford to pay for not one, but *two* damn residences, and I was struggling to keep up with one.

"Are you serious?" I squinted. "Who are you?"

"I'm Skoby Twan Paul. Now go pack your stuff." He leaned back in the chair and pulled his cell out of his pocket. "You need help with that too?" He asked sarcastically, peeping up at me from his lit phone screen.

"Fuck you!" I shot him the rod, slipping the key into my pocket and sliding off to my bedroom to pack up my things.

As expected, the apartment was a nice as his home. The décor was a lot softer, though. Pale yellow, peach, and a crazy blend of gray and purple that I don't think I'd ever seen. I packed lite, having no plans of staying there longer than it would take to find an apartment of my own. But I'd be lying if I said the place wasn't cozy as fuck. I could literally see Houston's skyline from the master bedroom window.

For reasons that could only be the result of my coldness and fragility in the last few weeks, Skoby was keeping his distance and letting me feel the place out. He sat in the living room, busying himself with text messages, social media, or whatever he did when

I wasn't right in front of his face. And I appreciated that for the first fifteen minutes. But then shit got awkward. Like was I supposed to ask him to stay or was he gonna bounce and leave me in this strange but cozy apartment alone?

"So, is this ok?" His voice pulled me outta my thoughts, standing in the doorway of the bedroom I'd be sleeping in, catching me sitting on the edge of the king-sized bed running my palms over the cool gray sheets.

"Yeah. It's… it's nice." I looked up at him leaning against the door trim.

"What was that?" His head went to the side.

"What was what?" I shrugged and looked over my shoulder.

"That hesitance. What's wrong?" He asked, stepping into the room and taking a seat beside me on the bed, causing it to dip.

"Nothin'." I lied as his shoulder brushed mine. "I just…"

"Just say it. Is the skyline too much? You scared of heights?"

"No!" I smiled.

"Then what is it?" He nudged my arm. "And don't say nothin' again."

"Could you stay?" I asked, looking up into his eyes. "I know you got stuff to do. But I was just—"

With his hand sliding up the side of my face, he pulled me into a kiss that melted every word from my lips. My nipples hardened, heart started pounding, and heat raced down between my legs. Autonomously, I turned my body into the groove of his side until he gripped the outside of my thigh and pulled me onto his lap.

"That's not what I meant!" I pulled away from a kiss, biting down on my lip and staring into his eyes, giving into a smile when he popped me on the ass.

"I bet this was your plan all along!" My breathing quickened as he kicked off his shoes and unbuckled his jeans.

"You got a problem with that?" He breathed against my neck, working his pants down and off. "Cause I can stop." He raised his head to look me right in the face, knowing damn well that wasn't about to happen.

I grabbed the hem of my T shirt, ripping it off over my head, exposing the less than sexy bra that I'd been putting on after showers for the last three days. Skoby didn't seem to mind the wilting, red rosettes. That is until he reached around my back to unhook all three prongs without ever taking his eyes off me.

The brother had pitched a tent under his boxers, and it was pressing against my behind. I reached down to stroke it but he quickly grabbed my hand, draping both my arms over his shoulders and whispering in my ear, "Slow down Lil Mama!"

Fucking tease.

I breathed in. The warmth from his breath on my skin was almost enough to make me come unglued. Then he sucked my neck, nipples smashed against the coolness of the T shirt he was still wearing. I rocked and rolled against his throbbing dick, pussy lips so swollen I thought they might pop. Skoby gripped his hands on either side of my waist, leaning me back so that my nipples were pointing at the ceiling. And I let him. Resistance was a thing I knew nothing about when his hands were on me. I felt a thick digit sweeping my panties to the side and held my breath until he was pushing inside of me.

"Fuck!" I moaned. The pressure of his thickness sliding between my slick folds forced me to arch my back and receive as much of him as I could, sending my breasts bouncing toward my chin then toward my navel. I tightened my legs around his waist with blood rushing to my head from being fucked nearly upside down. He slid in and out of me with a rhythmic stroke, big strong hands holding and controlling me, dark eyes piercing straight through my soul and assuring me that he wouldn't let me fall.

Almost completely taken over by dizziness, I gripped his forearms and lifted my head. Skoby's stare alone was enough to make me cum. The way he bathed me with his eyes, taking in my softness laying vulnerable in his hold. I could almost read his mind as he pushed deep inside me and pulled back just enough to gain more momentum and shove right back into me again.

He sat me up so that we were face to face, reaching up and pulling my hair from the knot I'd gathered it into. He loved it when it was hanging free, gripping it in his hands and tugging at it, pulling my head back as he pressed his lips to mine and slipped his tongue into my mouth. The sweet and salty taste of the meal we'd just shared lingered on his warm tongue, bathing my pallet and sucking me deeper into this kiss, hands enveloping my hips as I grinded hard against him. Taken over by the need to feel his skin against my skin, I hesitantly pulled away from his lips long enough to pull off his shirt. He was so fucking fine. Chest covered in ink that told stories I hadn't yet heard but couldn't wait to hear about, because in this moment, feeling as good as I felt, I couldn't imagine there was anything about this man I didn't wanna know. I smashed my lips right back into his, not even close to having enough of his tongue in my mouth. I roped my arms around his neck and stroked the short locks at the top of his tapered fade. Skoby was so deep in my pussy at this point that I could feel him in my belly.

After sucking away from my tongue, he traveled down to my nipples, suckling each one with the same vigor while I rolled my pussy over him again and again. Bringing me to the brink of climax, he dragged his teeth over each of my nipples before returning his eyes to mine, biting down on his bottom lip, gripping my waist tight and bouncing me up and down his length faster.

"Shit!" His eyes blinked closed, strokes intensifying, nails digging into my skin. Then he looked at me again, asking me without saying a word if it was okay to cum. Feeling the tingle and heat of my own climax arriving, clitoris swollen with the need to release, I tightened my walls around him and gripped my legs tighter around his waist. Pulling us closer together, so close that my nipples were smashed against is ripped chest, I wrapped my arms around his neck, bracing my palms at the back of his head, and rolled my hips against him until both of us were succumbing to an eruption of lust.

Eleven

Skoby

It had taken everything in me to leave her sleeping in that bed, after a night of exploring each other's bodies and not much else. Would've been perfect to wake up with her hair in my face, pretty brown thigh draped across me, and the sound of that goofy ass laugh when I popped her on her ass before rolling outta bed for breakfast. I wasn't sure if I would ever get enough of Joletta Rene Foster. I'd never considered myself an addict of anything until she landed in my path.

Or had I landed it in hers?

It was damn near impossible to tell.

Whatever the case, she had me off of my game. Rushing through meetings to make sure she was okay. Leaving my phone in the car to stop myself from hitting her up just to hear her voice. I was simping hard as fuck and being called out on it daily. It's like I wasn't even me no more. This wild haired chocolate woman had me gone.

"Green or yellow?" I'd heard my assistant, Yoni, talking but was too preoccupied with a grocery list from Jo to pay attention.

"My bad. Wassup?" I looked up from my phone.

"The fifth truck. You want it to be green or yellow?" She said, typing away at whatever project me and Smitty had dropped on her desk.

Yoni was thirty-five raising six kids on her own, and I have no idea how she balanced all that and still came to work with enough energy to manage the office. But she did. We'd hired her through the same agency we were partnering with for the job fair, which catered to folks in the same underprivileged areas we were building produce shops in. To date, Yoni was our biggest success story. In a span of five years, she'd gone from sleeping under a bridge while her kids were scattered around living with relatives, to now managing our home office and more importantly, earning enough to provide food, shelter, and stability for her kids. After finding out about my grandfather giving away fruits and vegetables back in the day, it made sense that I'd come out of my lost times with the desire to be charitable. It was the direct result of being raised by a man who gave without needing to be praised or even acknowledged. I was without a doubt a reflection of all that he was.

"Green." I said, dropping my phone in my pants pocket after replying to Jo's text. "Is that all, boss?" I joked, stretching my legs, sitting on the other side of her desk instead of mine across the hall, because in all honesty, she was the one keeping the office running like a well-oiled machine five days a week.

"It *ain't*." She rolled her moon shaped, cinnamon brown eyes up from her computer screen. "But given your condition, I won't put too much on you." She huffed out half a chuckle, full glossed lips curving.

"*Condition*?" I asked. "The hell you talkin about, Yoni?"

She halted her typing to say, "Rumor has it you got *the bug*."

"Just had a check-up yesterday. Clean bill of health over here."

"Not that kinda bug, fool. The love bug!" She smiled. "You know Smitty can't hold water. Said some pretty young thang got your nose wide open. When do I get to meet her?" She went back to typing one million words per minute, pausing for a second to pop a grape in her mouth. Yoni was full-figured and wore it well. But she went on a diet every other month and was done with it within seven days.

"You two hens should know that discussing my personal life at the office is malicious gossip, and you can jot that down for the next quarterly meeting." I joked, sliding forward in my seat.

"Malicious gossip or not, it's the truth based on the smile on your face every time you pick up that phone!" She followed me with her eyes as I left my seat and made my way to her open office door. "Don't run now, Mr. Lover Man!" She laughed.

"Ain't nobody runnin, man." I grinned. "You and Smitty need to find y'all some business." I tipped my chin and tapped the back of her chair on my way out of the office.

"Oh, we found some!" She yelled over her shoulder. "Gone get us another *Paul's Freshest* baby around here!" I heard her laughing out loud. Kerri probably still had gift cards from the baby shower Yoni put together at the office when Krissi was born. The woman lived for anything pertaining to children.

"Jo, where you at? I got greens, beans, tomatoes, potatoes, lamb ram. You naaaame it!" I put the groceries down on top of the kitchen counter and headed to the bedroom looking for Jo.

I didn't find her. But what I did find on top of one of the pillows was a pair of panties and a note addressed to me. It simply read,

I appreciate everything you've done for me, but these ain't my fuckin' panties. The key's under the rug.

Lose my number,

Jo

I didn't need to look at the panties twice to know who they belonged to. I'd seen Kerri prance around in em so many times she might as well have been in em right then. Better judgement had told me to let Jo know what was up with the apartment from the jump, but she was in a fragile space. I didn't wanna rock the boat with old bullshit that honestly didn't mean shit to me.

Guess I shoulda thought that out a little longer.

Ignoring the last line from the note, I pulled my phone out and called her anyway.

Blocked.

It's like I was taking two steps forward and twenty steps back with this woman. But even with all the frustration of having to explain myself when I'd never considered doing that for any other female, I wasn't at all turned off. The fact that she was mad about the possibility of me entertaining other chicks was proof that she felt more for me than she was letting on. The shit was beyond getting sexed crazy. Jo's mean ass was falling too.

I pulled up at the house just in time to catch Kerri getting ready to leave after dropping Krissi off without hitting me up first. She'd been dodging me since that day I dropped six bills to get my baby from a sitter that I knew nothing about, and Gams was stepping in to keep the peace, communicating with Kerri on my behalf and making sure Krissi came to my house rather than some random person when her mama wanted to hit the streets and do her thing. Truth be told, it was better if I didn't have to see Kerri's face. I had so much shit on my chest dealing with this girl and how she couldn't turn down long enough to read her daughter a bedtime story. But tonight, there was no way around it. At the worst possible time, I was gonna have to have it out with her.

"Wassup?" I tipped my head up, standing in front of Kerri, surprised that she'd waited for me to come back out.

"Nothing. I just… Can we talk?" Her voice sounded strained. Almost like she'd been crying.

"Yeah. You good?" I squinted, motioning for her to come take a seat in the living room just right of the entrance.

"Yeah, I'm… I'm fine. Just needed to run something by you. I already talked to Gams." She refused the seat and stood there with her arms folded across her ample chest.

"Talked to Gams about what? Krissi good?" I felt myself losing patience. "What's goin' on?"

"Skoby, I'm tired." She said, unfolding her arms.

"What you mean *tired*? You thinkin' bout killin' ya self or somethin'?" I stepped in closer and looked her straight in eyes. Just because I wasn't in love with Kerri didn't mean I didn't care about her well-being.

"What? No! *Never!*" Her eyes widened. "Good to see you give a fuck, though." Her stare softened. It was dangerous to show any signs of sympathy with this woman, cause she still wasn't over me and probably never would be.

I backed away a step or two to make it clear that I was only being human, not entertaining the whole *getting back together* shit. And she got the hint, I guess. Folding her arms back across her chest before continuing with what she had to say.

"We never talked about the whole thing with Krissi being left at the babysitter's."

"You mean the one I didn't know?" I cut in.

"Yeah, *that* one." She rolled her eyes.

"Ain't too much to talk about." I said. "She comes here now. No matter what you got going on or where you got it going on at, you bring my daughter here. Understand?"

"Skoby, why you always gotta talk to me like that?" She raised her voice. "I'm tryna have an adult conversation with you about our daughter and you acting like I'm a fucking child." She looked over my shoulder in the direction of Krissi's room and lowered her voice.

"Cause you do childish shit. Like leaving my daughter with strangers when she got a perfectly safe roof to lay under over here."

"Then why don't you keep her, then!?" She spat, voice shivering like she wasn't sure she'd wanted to say that shit out loud.

"You serious?"

"*Dead* serious." She replied. "I'm tired, Skoby. I love my baby with all my heart but I'm tired."

"Tired of what, Kerri? Half the time you don't even have her. What, she keeping you out the streets? Out these lame nigga's beds?"

"You used to *be* one of those lame niggas, Bee. So don't come at me with your fake ass judgment!"

"I ain't never been a lame nigga. So, watch ya mouth."

"Or what? You gone hit me?" She stepped up in my face, so close that I could feel the warmth from her nostrils on my chin.

"You'd like that shit, wouldn't you?" I glared down into her eyes. "That's how you communicate. With niggas' hands around ya neck."

"You ain't never been man enough to handle me." She stared at me with her lips trembling, so pissed that she probably would've thrown a punch if she didn't know I'd catch her fist mid-air.

"Get the fuck out my face, Kerri." I kept my tone even, aware that my baby was on the other side of the wall and could hear everything we were saying if she was awake.

"You forced this on me!" She didn't back away. "I told you I didn't want a baby and you talked me into keeping her. This shit is your fault!" She pointed her finger in my face.

130

"You need to go." I stepped back, and she took the step with me.

"Oh, I'm *gonna* go." She hissed. "And I'm not coming back. Tell Krissi that, since you were the one who wanted her so bad!"

"Why are you crying, Mama?" Krissi's little voice shocked us both as she walked out of her room and started walking toward us.

"Hey, Ladybug!" Kerri tried to lighten her voice. But the tears she palmed away had already been seen. "It's just allergies. Mama's okay." She stooped down and lied. And I wasn't experienced enough with this kind of situation to add anything to the conversation.

"Uncle Lemon has allergies. You want me to see if he has some medicine?" She asked, rubbing her mama's cheeks. Krissi had to be the most nurturing little girl I knew. Always tryna look out for somebody.

"No, baby. I'm okay." She grabbed both of Krissi's hands and kissed them one by one. "Why don't you go back to bed, okay? It's getting late."

"But I'm not sleepy." Krissi whined. "Are you gonna come stay with Daddy?" She asked.

"No, Krissi." I answered for her. As far as I was concerned, Krissi was old enough to understand that me and Kerri weren't together and wouldn't ever be together. We didn't have to be to love her.

"Go sit with Gams and Uncle Lem. Me and Mama need to finish talking." I ruffled my fingers through her hair and she bounced off to the other living room where Uncle Lem and Gams were sitting.

I waited until my daughter was out of earshot before asking, "Have you lost your damn mind? You can't just run off into the sunset like you ain't got no responsibilities."

"And why not? She got you. She got Gams and Uncle Lem."

"Cause you're her fucking mother, Kerri!" I raised my voice just loud enough to get the point across. "Listen I get it." I breathed out, trying my best to find a way to resolve this shit peacefully. Because as much as I resented Kerri for being the way she was, I loved by daughter more and couldn't imagine having to explain her mother's absence.

"But you don't." She shook her head. "You don't understand carrying a baby that you don't want, for nine months to satisfy a man that you'll never be good enough for. How the fuck could you possibly understand that?"

"You can throw that shit in my face til the cows come home, but that don't change the fact that Krissi's here."

"Nor does it change the fact that I'm not ready to be her mother." She snapped.

"Then who's supposed to do it?" I asked, hands shoved in my pockets because I didn't know what else to do with em. "I can be her father but I can't be you."

"Why don't you ask your little girlfriend?" She tilted her head to the side.

I knew this shit was coming.

"Must be love." She huffed. "I can't leave her with a babysitter that you don't know, but you can have her up in here making pancakes with a bitch I ain't never met? Crazy how the rules work when you makin' all of em."

"Change the subject all you want." I wasn't falling into that trap. "Still ain't no excuse for abandoning your child."

"I'm not abandoning her!" She argued.

"Then what do you call it?" I fumed. "Do you know how it feels to have your mama here one day and gone the next? You ever felt that shit?"

"You know I have!" She whimpered. "You know what I've been through, and it didn't affect me the way it affected you. That shit didn't make me a stronger person, Skoby. Not the type that can raise a little girl. That's why I didn't want kids. I don't know what the fuck I'm doing half the time, and it takes everything in me to get up every morning and show her love when that's a foreign fucking language to me!"

"But you do it." I looked Kerri in the eyes. Not just *through* her like I'd been doing since we split. But at her. Like a human. Like the mother of my child.

"I know I be on some bullshit with you." I said. "Mostly because we ain't compatible, and that's fucked up but it's life. But I can't let you give up on Krissi. No matter how I feel about the shit you got goin' on, she don't deserve that and neither do you."

The words came out of my mouth so fast, I almost didn't believe it was my voice speaking. Having at least an ounce of decency in my body, I pulled Kerri into a tight hug, her tears staining the front of my shirt while she wept. "You can do this shit, man." I rubbed her back. "You gotta man up!" I joked to lighten the mood.

"You stupid!" She chuckled, a strange reaction for both of us.

"You know I got her though, right?" I pushed her away at the shoulders and looked down into her eyes. "Whatever you gotta do to figure shit out, do that. But then come back. Ain't nobody tryna replace you."

"I know that."

"But do you?"

"I do!" She bucked her eyes. "I still don't have to like the bitch, though."

"Man, chill." I backed up to lean my back against the wall.

"Oh, so there is somebody?" She took a deep breath in, a smirk crossing her face.

"You worried about the wrong thing."

"When do I get to meet her?" She tilted her head to the side, propping a hand on her hip, wearing a pair of jeans that might as well have been a second skin.

"Where you gone be?" I ignored her question.

"So, you ain't answerin' my question?" She shifted her weight to the other hip. I sighed, eyes up to the ceiling.

"Whatever." She accepted that poking the bear wasn't gonna work that night. "I'll be in Killeen at Sheldon's. She got a job lined up for me."

"You couldn't find a job down here?" I asked.

"I need a change of scenery." She replied.

"Then what, you gone move Krissi up there?"

"Taking Krissi wasn't part of the plan."

"And now it *is*. So, what are you gonna do?"

"Look, can you just let me breathe?" She put both hands up, stepping toward the door. "I just told you I'm tired. I need time."

"Bet." I stood from leaning against the wall. "Take all the time you need." I walked past her and headed toward my room. "You can let yourself out!" I said without looking back. There was only so much talking I could do before compassion turned into frustration.

I went into my room and took a hot shower to calm down before I joined the two old folks and my baby in the living room. Gams and Uncle Lem were playing a hand of Pity Pat and cursing each other out as usual, while Krissi lay sprawled out asleep on one end of the sectional, oblivious to the fact that her little life was so damn complicated. I'd do all I could to protect that little girl from any kind of heart break. I didn't know how we were gonna maneuver through this shit, but the clock started ticking the second Kerri walked out the door.

"Lemont, you know damn well that ain't no two!" Gams fussed. Neither of em were wearing their reading glasses. This game was gonna go on until sun-up.

"That *is* a two!" Uncle Lem protested. "I'm lookin' right at it." He squinted at the card on top of the stack.

"Boy, that's a five! Tell him, Skoby." Gams looked up at me as I leaned against the back of Uncle Lem's chair.

"That's not a five, Gams." I shook my head.

"See, I told you that's a two. Pity Pat!" Uncle Lem threw his whole hand down and scooped about five dollars' worth of quarters from the center of the coffee table.

"It's not a two either, Unc." I chuckled. "That's an eight, man. Y'all been drinkin'?" I took a seat on the sofa next to Gams, stretched out my legs and pulled my hands behind my head.

"Well I'll be damned." Gams picked up the card like she should have in the first place. "Do they make these things any bigger? This shit is too little!" She flipped the card front to back, then dropped it on the table and fell back against the couch.

"Cards ain't worth a shit!" Uncle Lem huffed, swiping a hand at the cards and sitting back in his seat.

"What you doin' in so early?" Gams asked. "Jo ran you off?"

"Somethin' like that." I breathed out.

"Aww shit." Uncle Lem popped his thigh.

"What's that for?" Gams eyed Uncle Lem.

"Trouble in paradise. That's what." Uncle Lem replied. "I knew you wasn't draggin' them long ass legs in her for nothin'. What you do?"

"What? Nothin'." I lied. "What makes you think I did somethin'? I can't just chill with y'all? Help y'all see numbers and shit?"

"Oh yeah, you definitely fulla shit now." Gams chimed in.

"Up to the neck." Uncle Lem added, bringing a straightened palm to his neck.

"Come off it, Bee. What's goin' on?" Gams pressed.

"It's nothin'." I said. "Jo's trippin', and now this mess with Kerri." I added on a sigh.

"Don't even mention that." Gams threw a hand up. "Saw it comin' the day she came home from the hospital with that baby. And I know ain't nobody perfect, but I sleep a lot better with Krissi under this roof."

"Can't say I disagree." I said. "That's still her mama though. She can't just burn off."

"Well, it ain't foreign in that family." Gams noted, pulling a blanket down over Krissi's feet. "Kerri's mama wasn't worth two nickels rubbed together. Ain't no tellin' what that girl done seen and been through."

"I know." I breathed out. "I'm just tryna do what's best for Krissi."

"I understand." She replied. "And as hard as it is to accept, sometimes the best thing to do for your baby might hurt her a little at first. Krissi'll be fine whether her mama comes back or not. It ain't your job to make her stay. It's your job to be here for this baby either way. You understand me?"

"Yes ma'am." I nodded, feeling like a five-year-old that had just been told that I could have ice cream after an ass whooping.

"Good. Now what did you do to Jo? You tried to fuck her didn't you?" Gams got way too hype. "I knew it. You just couldn't wait to bring that ole ding-a-ling in the picture. Skoby, you can't fuck everybody you meet. Sometimes it's better to take things slow."

I couldn't catch my breath fast enough to respond to the fact that my grandma was openly discussing my sex life. The shit blew my mind. I mean nothing was off limits with me and Gams, but she had never came at me like that.

"It ain't my business to tell, but that ship sailed a long time ago, Jules." Uncle Lem was ratting me out right in front of my face. There was some cold-blooded shit going down in my living room.

"Unc, for real!?" I threw both hands up in the air. "Y'all wildin', man."

"Oh, he ain't tellin' me nothin' new." Gams waved a hand. "Thought I was imaging that fresh-fucked glow on your faces the other day when we cooked breakfast together. Looks like I was right." She folded her arms across her chest.

"Umm hmm." Uncle Lem added.

"So, what'd you do to run her off? I can't wait to hear this." Gams crossed her feet at the ankles, wearing a pair of fuzzy pink socks that Krissi had bought for her last Christmas.

"Remember the apartment me and Kerri had together?" I started. Didn't even bother defending myself.

"Yeah. You let her keep it when you bought the house, right?" Gams noted.

"Yes ma'am." I said. "Well Kerri moved out almost a year ago, but I was still paying rent cause the lease ain't up for like three months."

"And? What does that have to do with Jo?" Gams asked.

"He done moved her in." Uncle Lem chirped. "Didn't you?" He cut his eyes at me.

"I did." I said, watching Gams's mouth fall open. "She was having a hard time sleeping at the house her and her grandma had lived in. I was just tryna help, and she winds up finding a pair of panties that Kerri left behind."

"Did you tell her who used to live there?" Gams asked.

"I tried but she blocked me."

"Why didn't you bring her here?" Gam's asked. "You got three empty bedrooms; not that she'd make it past yours!"

"Gams, lemme make it, man!" I chuckled. "And you know I woulda brought her here, but she didn't wanna be here like that with Krissi being around. Didn't wanna confuse her I guess."

"Well, that makes sense." Gams sighed. "She's smart, Bee. Way smarter than that damn gold diggin' baby mama."

"Gams?" I slanted my eyes at her.

"What? I'm just tellin' the truth. And if you woulda listened to me in the first place—"

"I know." I cut her off. "We had this talk before. Remember?"

"Hmpf." Her shoulders rose.

"Obviously, you ain't gone win this debate, nephew." Uncle Lem said. "Where's your girl and how do you plan on gettin' her back?"

"She ain't mine though, Unc." The taste of those words made my mouth dry.

"And she never will be with that defeatist attitude." Gams spoke up. "I done forgave alotta people for alotta things. One bein' the man sittin' in front of me for keepin' my husband out all times of the night lookin' for him under bridges and shit." She cut her eyes at Uncle Lem who'd long gotten over Gams's smart mouth, and wasn't the least bit bothered by it.

"But I won't forgive you if you don't figure out a way to get to that girl." She continued. "I haven't seen you light up like this since the day you brought Krissi home from the hospital. And you might not see it, cause you ain't lookin' from eyes of experience, but she lights up the same way as soon as you walk in the room."

Gams hit me with a load of something I wasn't expecting. There were plenty of times when I didn't think things were gonna work out and had to take her word for it. Seemed like now was gonna be one of those times.

"Come on, I'll drive you to her house." Uncle Lem stood from his seat, snatching his keys off the side table. "What you waitin' on? You scared?" He asked when I didn't join him.

"She ain't there." I said. "Drove by on my way home and all the lights were off."

"Well where else would she be?" Gams asked.

"I don't know her well enough to know that. But she ain't friendly."

"Who was the bartender lady she was workin' for? Seemed like they were pretty good friends." Uncle Lem reminded me. And he was right. Vanessa was the one who'd called to let me know about Mama Jo, and she'd for sure know where to find this woman I couldn't seem to stop chasing.

Without a second thought, I hit Vanessa up, crossing my fingers that she'd answer and tell me she knew where I could find this wild-haired woman who was turning my world upside-down. It was just my luck that she answered on the second ring, giving me attitude nonetheless. But I'd take what I could get.

"Hey, *Vanessa*?" I said.

"This is she." She replied.

Dry as fuck.

"I hate to bring you in the middle of this, but I don't know how else to—"

"You got some balls calling my phone for a woman who obviously wants nothing to do with you." She cut me off.

"Listen, I know Jo probably told you some foul shit about me, but if she'd just let me explain." Pleading to a woman was a foreign to me as speaking Mandarin. But again, I was doing what I had to do.

"Explain what?" She hissed. "How you had my girl living in your jump-off spot? Oh, I would love to hear you elaborate on this!"

I breathed in and channeled the nice nigga that lived somewhere deep down in my chest so he could complete this conversation. "I'd rather explain it to Jo, but if I gotta go through security first, that's fine." I joked. She laughed, but I got the feeling she didn't find the shit funny.

After a few minutes of hearing my side, she told me that Jo was at her place, shot me her address, and promised not to tell her I was on my way. I was surprised as shit that she believed what I told her, and honestly a little hesitant to drive over, thinking maybe I was being set up. Women do crazy shit for their home girls. But I went with it. So desperate to see her face, that I'd've flown to the moon to tell her just that. Uncle Lem wanted to drive me but I told him to chill. There were certain things a man had to go get on his own.

Twelve

Skoby

I pulled up to Vanessa's apartment complex about a quarter to nine, a nice high rise with reserved parking and a doorman who wouldn't even touch the door unless the resident knew your name. I thought about stopping to grab an order of our sweet and salty mix. But I was so in a rush to fix this shit that I didn't even have an appetite.

The glass elevator that I was directed to by the narrow-nosed doorman who refused my tip, gave a full view of the modern designed complex as I rode to the fifth floor, reciting lines like I was auditioning for a movie. I'd had it perfectly memorized by the time I reached Vanessa's apartment door, but when she opened it and I saw the back of Jo's head sitting on her sofa, all that shit went out the window, and all I wanted to do was kiss her neck.

"Is that the pizza? I'm starving." Jo said, eyes glued to the TV without looking back.

"She ain't even trippin." I said to myself. *"I'm standing here with no fucking appetite and she's watching TV and waiting on pizza."*

"You know what, my bad." I whispered, backing away from the door.

"What? No!" Vanessa whispered back.

"Thanks. But this was a bad idea." I took another step back and was about to turn and walk away until she grabbed the sleeve of my hoodie.

"Wait!" She said, reaching back and pulling the door closed behind her. "She might look like she's okay, but she's not." She said, eyes widening as she stood in front of me barefoot in the carpeted hallway.

I breathed in and slid my hands in my pockets, still not sure if I was making the right decision. What if she still wasn't tryna hear me? What if the circumstances didn't matter and she was just using it as an excuse to push me away?

"Look, I barely know her." I said. Vanessa stood there with her arms folded across her chest. Little light skinned shorty was the Gina to Jo's Pam.

"Yeah? Well, that's where I come in." She leaned her head to the side. "She was hurt about the shit. Hell, Jo's hurt about alotta shit. She wouldna stormed off and chose to sleep on my couch if she wasn't. That's just how she operates."

"I get that." I said. "And I know she's ya girl and everything, but we ain't been kickin' it that long."

"You could've been kickin' it five years and Jo wouldn't speak your name if she wasn't feeling you." She said, shifting her weight to one slender hip. "But that's not the case." She sighed. "She might have your number blocked, but she's been stalking your social media pages for the past few hours between episodes of *Grey's Anatomy*. And word of advice, you need to post more often cause you're inactive as fuck for a business tycoon."

She dropped her arms and turned back to the door, twisting the knob and pushing it open. "You coming to get your woman or not? She's wearing a groove in my fucking couch."

Vanessa was funny as shit. I could see why Jo had her as a friend.

"Damn, you gotta suck his dick for the pizza or somethin'? I'm starving!" Jo joked, turning around and looking over the back of the couch. Her mouth dropped when she saw me standing there.

"Are you fucking serious, Vanessa?" She pushed a blanket off her lap and stood from the sofa. "I don't have *shit* to say to you." She rolled her eyes at me and stormed out of the living room, passed me by and hurried down a short hallway.

"Second room on the right." Vanessa pointed me in the direction that Jo had traveled. "Go. Don't think, just go!" She locked the front door and pranced over to the living room where Jo had been sitting, smirking back at me over her shoulder.

With my next breath lodged in my throat, a slumped down the hallway until I reached the second room on the right.

Do I knock?

Do I push it open?

Do I stand there until she comes out with a can of mace?

I decided against all that and simply spoke her name.

"Jo." I stood directly in front of the door with my hands still in my pockets. "I know you ain't tryna hear it but I just wanted to set things straight." I said, not knowing if she could hear me or was even listening.

"I shoulda told you what was up with the apartment, but I was just tryna... I just wanted to make sure you were okay. I know what you were going through—*are* going through—and I didn't think. I just acted."

I stopped for a minute to gather myself. Didn't know what to say next, but felt like more needed to be said. Why'd this shit have to be so complicated? I was doing the right thing—what my grandfather would've done. She needed a place to go and I gave her that. Why'd it matter that my fucking baby's mama once slept in the same bed?

The sheets were clean.

"The panties were Krissi's mama's." I continued, stupidly feeling the need to keep moving my lips instead of shutting up and heading for the door before I made shit worse. "She stayed there for a—*we* stayed there for a while. I was tryna make it work for Krissi but it... it just... it didn't. I moved out and let her keep the place til she got on her feet, and I guess she left some stuff behind. I'm sorry I didn't tell you that in the first place. I didn't think it was a big deal."

"Cause you're stupid." She said. But her voice came from behind me instead of the room.

I turned around and said, "She told me you were in—"

"I had to pee." She cut me off. "I've been sitting on that couch drinking wine coolers and watching the longest fucking medical drama known to man, and I couldn't hold it no more."

She pulled a band off her wrist and pulled her hair up into a knot on top of her head. She had to know I hated that shit. Was she tryna get her lick back?

"Well?" She dropped her arms to the side after securing the knot.

"Well what?" I squinted. "You tryna box or somethin'? Pullin' your hair up and shit?"

"I'm not in the mood for joking, Skoby. You put me up in you and your baby mama's old apartment and didn't think that was something I needed to know? You fucked me in the same bed you fucked her in."

"Would it have mattered?" I asked, pulling my hands from my pockets.

"What?"

"You heard me. Would it have made a difference if I told you who stayed there before? She ain't there no more, Jo."

"Hell yeah, it would've mattered!" Her brows and voice hiked. "And you know it. That's why you fuckin' lied."

"I didn't lie."

"But you didn't exactly tell the truth. And from where I'm standing, that looks like the same thing."

I couldn't debate that. Probably wouldn't win if I did. So, I said, "I'm sorry."

"You said that already."

"And I'm saying it again."

"But that doesn't fix it."

"Then what will?!" I raised my voice.

Fuck, I didn't mean to raise my voice.

"What other secrets are you keeping from me?" She asked. "Is some girl on the other side of town waiting for you to drop by with this same apology? Were her panties in one of the drawers I didn't look in?"

I didn't answer either question, cause now she was being childish. And I'd entertain alotta shit with Jo, cause she had my head gone that bad. But childishness wasn't one of em. She had the wrong nigga for that.

"Must be true." She huffed. "Why are you here?" She sighed.

"Cause *you're* here. You already know that."

"I don't know shit except that you must think I'm some simple bitch you can run game on."

"Ain't nobody runnin' game, Jo. I told you what was up and you ain't tryna hear it."

"Then why you still here?" She got up in my face, the soft scent of vanilla body wash rising from her skin like scented hypnosis.

"Cause you haven't asked me to leave." I replied, looking

down into her eyes, daring her to look away, walk away, or push me away.

"It was a mistake—*my* mistake—moving you in that apartment without telling you everything. But I'm not about to keep apologizing when all I was tryna do was look out for your stubborn ass. And I'm sure as hell not apologizing for whatever females you think I'm entertaining when it's clear to everybody but you that I ain't got time for nobody else."

I was speaking so close to her face that my breath was blowing the wild hair that hung against her forehead. Jo stood as still as a statue. Didn't even flinch while I was speaking. I couldn't tell if she was about to cry or curse me the fuck out. But tears were welling in her eyes, and that had me feeling like the weakest nigga in the world.

"I don't give a fuck what's clear to everybody else!" She said, lips trembling.

"Jo..."

"Don't!" She put a finger to my lips. "We can go in circles all damn night, but it won't change the fact that you don't understand what I'm tryna say."

"Jo—"

"I cannot tolerate secrets, lies, or you keeping shit from me to save my feelings, Skoby." She cut me off again, tears streaming down her cheeks like rain. "I just lost my Mama. I am literally standing in front of you tryna figure out what the fuck I'm supposed to do with myself now that she's gone. And all you can do is keep telling me how sorry you are for being a fucking idiot. A fucking *idiot*, Skoby! You laid me in that bed and made love to me. *Love*! And I don't think I've ever felt that in any man's arms. So when you tell me that you're sorry about inviting me into a home you shared with another woman, after worshipping my pussy like God himself led you to do so, I have to question my feelings. I have to question my judgement. I have to question every minute

146

I've spent with you since the day you decided that with you is where I'm supposed to be. And you can't apologize for that."

"But I—"

"Don't fucking tell me you're sorry again!" She screamed so loud I almost jumped. "Just leave. And take your apologies with you!"

There weren't enough words in my vocab to describe how twisted I felt. Crying wasn't an option for me at this point, because she was so far from forgiveness that she couldn't even see straight. I stood there for a moment staring down at her as she struggled to catch her breath. Jo was hurting, and it was apparent that the pain she was feeling had been building up before she even met me.

So, I left.

Without touching her, or kissing her, or holding her against my chest like I'd wanted to, I turned to walk away with a lump the size of Houston lodged in my throat. I'd lost all hope of mending this shit. She'd told me from her own lips that sorry wouldn't do. And to be honest, at the time, sorry was all I had.

Thirteen

Jo

As hard as it was to sit in that house, it was harder to keep sleeping on Nessa's hard ass sofa since she'd turned my old room into a home office. I could still feel Mama's spirit lingering around, worrying about whether I'd be alright, and trying her best to be there for me when she couldn't.

I still hadn't cried. Wouldn't let my thoughts go to the place where all those tears were sitting. And though the whole situation with Skoby had brought a few tears to my eyes, it was nowhere near as bad as I'd imagined it being if I ever mourned Mama. I wanted to release. Felt like I needed to because everything in my life was off balance at this point. I'd been back in Mama's house for a solid month, and aside from working at the *Big Reads*, I didn't have human contact with anybody but Aunt Janine and Nessa.

"Ma'am, can you help me?" A customer stepped up to the counter and snapped me out of my thoughts. "I was looking for a new line of children's books for my son. *The Awesome Adventures of Dyl and Dev?*"

"Yes ma'am, we carry those." I rounded the counter and extended my arm in the direction that she was to follow me in.

"Do you have kids?" The chipper, brown-skinned lady asked, following alongside me on our way to the children's section of the two-story book store that had been my place of peace before life got so messy.

"No ma'am." I looked to the side and smiled at her. "But I've read all the books. It's pretty neat to see two little black boys on book covers."

"I know, right!?" She said, voice bubbling with excitement. "My baby was so excited to get his hands on them. At first I thought he was begging for video games, but when he told me that Dyl and Dev were characters in a book, I almost broke my neck getting up here!"

I gave a kind nod, mustering all the positive energy I had left to be polite. "And here we are." I waved a hand over the display I'd put together that morning—life-sized cartoon cutouts of two little black boys. One with brown locs down to his shoulders, and another with a jet-black tapered fade. Dyl—the oldest of the adventurous duo—wore a grass-green shirt and blue jean pants. Dev—the younger brother—wore a bright yellow shirt with khaki pants. And both of them had on huge white tennis shoes that would be impossible to walk in, in real life.

"Is there anything else I can help you with?" I asked the lady as she sifted through the five-book series spread out on the long, rectangular table.

"Oh, no." She looked up and to the side at me. "Just tryna decide if I should start slow and get one, or go all in and get the whole set. What do you think?" She bit down on her pointer finger with one book in her hand already.

And being the salesperson that I was, I said "All I'm gonna say is that they go fast. If he's a fast reader, he'll be done with this one before the week ends. And every one of these babies ends on a cliffhanger."

"Are you serious? Is that how they doin' the kids?" She code switched. A sister had been living inside that head the whole time and she was hiding her from me.

"That's *exactly* how they doin' the kids!" I chuckled.

"Well in that case, let me save myself the trouble and get the whole set. Thank you, girl!" She quickly plucked four more books from the table and headed back toward the register.

I was about to head off behind her when a little voice caught my attention. "Jo!" She yelled. "Daddy, I told you that was Jo!"

The cutest little girl came running toward me at the speed of lightening and wrapped her arms around my thigh like she'd missed me or something.

"Hey, Krissi!" I patted her hair and looked down at her smiling. "I see you're keeping up with that hair, girl. You look so pretty!" She smiled so hard her eyes were squinting.

"Thank you!" She chirped. "What happened to your hair?" She asked. I always kept it pulled back into a knot for work. Plus my hair had to match my mood and I was feeling pulled back as fuck.

"I had a bad hair day." I said, noticing that Skoby was taking his time getting over to us. "It was good seeing you, Krissi. I gotta go help a customer. Let me know if you need help with anything okay?" I patted her head then tried to walk away, but she wouldn't loosen her hold on my leg.

"Krissi, I gotta go, baby." I spoke softly.

"Krissi, come on." Skoby waved a hand from where he was standing, less than twelve feet away. He looked as delicious as the last time I'd seen him. But not delicious enough to speak to.

"But you don't know where stuff is, Daddy." She fussed. "That's why you always put my books on the Kindle. But I want real books. You said I can get real books for my birthday, Daddy!"

"Ma'am, I don't mean to rush you but…" The Dyl and Dev lady shouted from the register.

"I'm so sorry, I'll be right there." I shouted back with Krissi still attached to my leg.

"But you have to help us first, Jo." Krissi looked up into my eyes. "Daddy said book stores are for old people. He don't even know where to find stuff."

"Ma'am, I have to pick my son up from daycare." The Dyl and Dev lady yelled again.

"I'm coming." I said, bracing my arms on Krissi's little shoulder and practically dragging her to the register.

"Krissi, come… Krissi come on." Skoby hopelessly pleaded with his little girl, hesitantly coming closer to us. Awkwardness was written all over his face.

"Jo's at work. She gotta help other customers." He said, now standing right next to us. So close that I could smell that got damn cologne. I had to take a deep breath to calm my insides.

"I'll get it." April, the only other associate on shift at the time intervened. "This looks like a really important customer!" She winked at Krissi.

"Thank you, April. Jo's my friend!" Krissi read April's nametag and nearly shocked the shoes off my feet.

"Wow! How'd you know my name?" April asked, smiling and nodding at the Dyl and Dev lady while ringing up her books.

"I read your nametag, silly!" She giggled. "I can read *anything*!" She let go of my leg long enough to clap her hands together, then latched right back onto it like a little spider.

"Come on, Jo! I need alotta books! Oooh, Dyl and Dev!" She looked to her right and took off toward the Dyl and Dev display, leaving me and her daddy standing there alone.

He didn't look worn, or tired, but he did look like he'd seen better days. I'm sure that he'd say the same about me if I'd asked. But I wasn't going to. In fact, I didn't have anything to say.

"Look, I didn't… I didn't know you worked here." He started, breaking the awkward silence. "We only come in here for birthdays. And it's usually her and Gams. So I…"

"It's fine." I said. "It's not like I own the place." I took off walking towards an excited Krissi, who'd already gathered up three out of five books from the Dyl and Dev collection.

"Daddy, can I get these!?" She squealed.

"Those're some big books, Kris. I'on't know." He rubbed two fingers down his bearded chin, stopping in front of the display and folding one arm across his chest, tucking a hand under his arm.

"But I have time to read. It's Christmas break, remember?" She kept pressing, looking up at the man whose chocolate skin tone she'd inherited, big kinky hair crowning her little head so perfectly.

"You got a point." He squinted. "How many books in this collection?" He asked me, knowing I wouldn't be a bitch in front of Krissi.

"Five." I answered without making eye contact, instead walking over to grab a handheld basket for Krissi to place her books in. "And they come with these Dyl and Dev bookmarks too!" I picked up two glossy bookmarks off the display table and dropped them in the basket that I placed in front of her.

"Cooool!" She smiled. "Do you get to read all these books, Jo? This is a dream job!" Her eyes ballooned as she took inventory of the book-covered space all around her.

"I can if I want to." I folded my arms and followed her hazel eyes. "But I've only read about five hundred."

"Five hundred books!? Oh my God!" Her eyes doubled in size.

"Yep, five hundred. And if you keep on reading, by the time you're my age, I bet you can beat that record." I ruffled my fingers through her hair, trying hard to ignore the fact that her daddy was standing there trying not to stare at me.

And he wasn't alone in that. All I'd wanted to do since the moment I saw him was ask if he was okay. If he'd moved on like he should, to someone less complicated that he didn't have to shelter and hide shit from.

But I knew he hadn't. Even though our courtship had been fast and intense, Skoby didn't strike me as the type to hop from chick to chick. At least not the same way he'd hopped on me.

As Krissi rattled on about all the books she'd read—quickly making it through all ten fingers—Skoby pulled a ringing phone from his pocket.

"Hey, you mind keeping an eye on her for a sec? I gotta take this." He said after looking up from the phone screen.

"Um… sure." I said. "Come on, let's go see what else we can find." I grabbed Krissi's hand while she lifted her basket from the table.

"Take your time, Daddy. *I'm in my zone!*" She deepened her voice. Skoby hissed out a chuckle, shaking his head and mouthing *"Thank you,"* as he resumed the call and headed toward the front of the store.

"Where'd you get that from?" I looked down at Krissi and asked.

"Get what from?" She looked up at me, bopping along in a rainbow tutu that matched her scarlet red turtle neck and yellow tights.

"I'm in my zone." I deepened my voice just like she had. "Where'd you hear that?"

"Oh!" She giggled. "Daddy says that when he's listening to music in his office. And then we dance!" She kicked up a little foot.

"Oh, I see." I smiled, ushering her to an aisle stocked full of children's books.

"We haven't danced in a long time. Since Mama dropped me off." She disclosed, putting her basket down on the floor.

"Really?" I shamelessly pried. "How long ago was that?" I didn't wanna know the answer. But Jesus, I did.

"I don't know." She said. "She didn't come to Thanksgiving, that's all *I* know." Her voice went up and she rolled her eyes. Krissi had so much personality for somebody so small.

"She called you though, right? To say gobble gobble?" I nudged her little shoulder as she pulled a bright pink book about princesses from the shelf and sat down on the floor with her legs crossed.

Krissi shook her head *no* without looking up from the book. I looked around before hesitantly getting down on the floor with her and crossing my legs too. Skoby hadn't said much about Krissi's mother. All I knew was that things hadn't worked out. That was it and that was all.

"Do you have a mama, Jo?" She looked up from the book, pretty little eyes so suddenly full of sadness.

"I did... I mean I *do*." I didn't know how to respond.

"It can't be both, silly!" She smiled.

And she was right. I either had a mama or I didn't.

"Did your daddy tell you about Mama Jo, my grandma?" I asked, for some reason sensing that he had.

"Yes, ma'am." She nodded. "He said she went to Heaven and you were sad, and that's why you don't come over anymore."

My mouth was open but no words were coming out. A lump lodged in my throat that would certainly break if I so much as attempted to speak.

"It's okay, Jo." Krissi raised up on her knees, roping her little arms around my neck and nestling my head against her chest like a woman seven times her age.

"I cried when my Mama left too. But I didn't tell Daddy or Uncle Lemon, cause boys can't handle stuff like that." She was dead-ass soothing me and I had no idea what to do.

So I cried.

And I laughed.

And I allowed Krissi to caress my back while squeezing me harder than any little girl should ever know how. I'd completely forgotten where I was. Books, customers, and job be damned. I was breaking down in this baby's arms. I was literally turning into a puddle.

"Jo, you alright?" Skoby's voice hovered over our heads. I felt like I'd been sitting on a cloud up until then.

And I still couldn't speak. My shoulders were jumping and my face was a wet mess, and so was the front of Krissi's shirt. I had no explanation as to what was going on. With every tear that fell, memories of Mama kept flooding my mind.

"She's crying, Daddy. Go do something until she gets finished." Krissi shooed her daddy away with a tiny hand.

"Crying for what? Jo, why you cryin'?" He stooped down on the floor behind Krissi and lifted my chin from her chest with the tips of his fingers.

With my chest heaving, lips trembling, and tears staining my face, I stuttered, "Mama! I miss my Mama!"

Five words had never been so hard to say. I thought I might die from all the sadness circling through my body. I felt Krissi's arms moving from around my back, and in one swift motion, Skoby had scooped me up off the floor.

Fourteen

Skoby

I'd given up on the idea of being with her—of her wanting to be with me. It wasn't the easiest decision I'd ever made, but I didn't have much of a choice in the matter. I'd deleted her number from my phone. Stopped stalking her social media. Even decorated the powder blue room that we'd made love in and turned it into a little home library for Krissi to put up all the books Gams said she needed.

Which was how I wound up in the bookstore, right back in her path without trying.

When me and Krissi turned the corner and saw Jo standing there in those khaki pants and that white Polo shirt, I had every intention of turning around and taking Krissi to another store, cause I didn't want Jo thinking I was a stalker or some shit. But once Krissi saw her *hair idol*, there was no escaping. She tore away from my hold faster than I could tell her not to.

"I'm sorry." She sniffled in the passenger seat of my truck. I'd carried her to the front of the store and squared things away with her manager, who said that it was almost the end of her shift and it was okay to take her home.

It must've been obvious to others that Jo hadn't grieved over Mama Jo. Even Vanessa had hit me up a couple of times since we split and told me so.

"You're good." I said, dragging my eyes from Jo to the road ahead of me. "You hungry? I can grab you somethin' to eat bef—"

"No." She whimpered. "I just wanna lay down."

Krissi had finally passed out in the backseat after I assured her that Jo would be okay. Even if I didn't know that to be true, I had to say it to my baby. She was always so in tune with people. Always had this healing quality about her, and I was afraid she might feel guilty if she hadn't helped Jo.

"Am I taking you home or—"

"Where else would you be taking me, Skoby?" She cut me off, keeping her voice low, well aware that Krissi picked up on everything. "Yes, home."

I took a deep breath in and turned up the music. It was apparent that she was no closer to forgiving me than she had been a month ago.

Roughly twenty minutes later, we pulled up to Jo's house. A sadness loomed over me just looking at the stoop where I'd last seen Mama Jo alive. And if what I was feeling was even a fraction of what Jo was feeling, there was no way she should be staying there alone.

"Jo." I let down the passenger side window as she stepped out without saying a word.

"What?" She turned around to look at me, eyes puffy from crying so much.

"We can stay a little while if you…"

"Go home, Skoby." Her eyes squinted and tears started to fall again. I hopped out of the truck before I knew it, and was standing right in front of her face.

"I know you hate me."

"I don't hate you." She cried. And I hated that shit. Hated it more than anything.

"Well, you don't *like* me." I returned. "And that's cool. I'm not tryna change that. I just know how it feels to lose somebody. To miss somebody that ain't never comin' back."

"Oh you do, do you?" She nodded her head, folding her arms across her chest.

"Yeah. I do." I replied, staring down into her eyes, remembering why the hell I missed her so much.

"I'm... I'm sorry. I didn't mean to—"

"No biggie." I shrugged. "Just know that I know. And you'll be alright. Look at *me*!" I spread my arms out to the side and smiled.

She wiped the tears from her eyes and let out a deep sigh, looking past the side of me as the door to my truck clicked open. "You should activate child-lock on those doors." She said, barely smiling as the pitter patter of Krissi's boots traveled in our direction.

"Jo, can I use your bathroom? I gotta pee like a race horse." Krissi said, embarrassing me like it was her job to do so.

"Krissi, can you hold it til we get home?" I offered, not wanting to impose.

"She's fine." Jo said, making her way to the door and unlocking it.

"You just gonna stand out here in the cold?" She slanted her eyes at me.

"I... uh—"

"I uh. Bring your behind on in here." She mocked me. "You're gonna freeze to death."

"It's like sixty-five degrees out. I doubt it." I walked up to the door and followed her in.

"It's Houston. That's basically an arctic blast." She joked. Hadn't seen that side of her in way too long.

Fifteen

Jo

"This is a nice ass house, Jo."

Nessa's ass was never impressed by anything, but she was smitten by all things related to Skoby Twan Paul.

"It's too big." I took my eyes up to the ceilings in the foyer that I'd visited on a few occasions. They were now trimmed with lit Christmas garland, as the Paul residence celebrated Christmas.

"No such thing." Nessa rolled her eyes, throwing back another swig of eggnog. And I prayed it wasn't spiked because she was the only bartender I knew who couldn't handle her liquor.

"Can we make that your last cup? You getting' kinda loud?" I suggested, taking the empty, eight ounce glass from her hand and directing her back into the party room where Gams was entertaining several guests.

"Kill joy!" She licked out her tongue, linking her arm through mine and hip bumping me as little Michael Jackson sang over the sound system about seeing his mama kissing Santa Claus.

"I'll be that." I bumped her back. "Can you handle yourself while I go find my little friend? She's been M.I.A for a while."

"Sure." She said. "Use that baby as an excuse to track down her daddy. I won't tell a soul!" Nessa pulled me to her side at the waist, then bumped me away as she joined the small crowd of family and friends, zooming in on Skoby's homeboy, Smitty.

Every part of the house was all decked out. Skoby was right when he said Gams didn't half-step on shit. It was literally a winter wonderland up in there, from the snowflakes hanging from the light fixtures, to the winter-blue stencil lining the baseboards. All of this had been put on for little Miss Krissi, who'd been in a funk after pulling me out of mine. I hadn't visited the house since Skoby carried me from the library, but Krissi demanded that we talk on the phone every single day, so she could make sure my voice didn't sound sad. It was because of those calls that I'd somewhat softened to Skoby. We were nowhere near dating, but at least on speaking terms. I wanted to drop my guard completely, mostly because I was horny as fuck and knew he could fix that with precision. But also because there was so much more I wanted to know about him and what made him the way that he was.

In any event, I was on a search for Krissi, and it didn't take long before I found her in the old powder blue room, that had been beautifully converted into a library fit for a princess.

"Hey, lil woman. What you doin' in here?" I peeped in through the open door to find her sitting on a round, sky blue rug with clouds on the perimeter, with her legs folded, reading a book.

"Reading." She said without looking up. And I could tell by the tremble in her voice that she was doing more than reading.

I took a deep breath and stepped into the room, popping a squat in front of Krissi and slipping a tear stained book from her tiny hands.

"That doesn't sound like a reading voice." I said. "And I bet this book didn't come with wet pages." I added, sitting the book down beside me.

"Talk to me. Tell me what's going on." I grabbed ahold of both her hands, so little and warm, with nails painted red.

"I didn't want Daddy and Uncle Lemon to see me cry." She looked up at me, eyes red from crying.

"Oh, Krissi! I bet they'd know what to do." I said.

"But they don't." She said, so sure of it.

"Well, who do you go to when you wanna cry? You gotta have somebody. Shoot, I had *you*!" I pinched her cheek, and she leaned her head on her shoulder smiling.

"I always go to Gams. But she can't be sad with me. She's hosting a Christmas party." She shrugged her drooping little shoulders. Her attitude didn't come close to matching the pretty red dress, matching red stockings, and grass-green patent leather shoes that Gams had, no doubt, picked out for her.

"I'll tell you what." I offered, scooting in closer with my legs folded to the side because the tight dress I was wearing didn't allow me to sit Indian style like Krissi. "Since you were there for me back at the library, how about I be here for you at this Christmas party? It can be our little secret. If you don't want me to tell Daddy and Uncle Lemon, I won't say a peep." I zipped my fingers across my lips.

Krissi nodded yes, and the cutest little smile spread across her face.

"Cool." I nodded in return. "But first you have to tell me what you're crying about."

She took a deep breath in—something I'd only seen grown-ups do. Then she said, "My mama was supposed to be here. Daddy let me talk to her on the phone and she said she'd be here for Christmas. But she didn't come, because she doesn't want me."

I knew that I was supposed to be the one holding Krissi while she cried, but as soon as I saw a tear slide down her cheek, I pulled her in against my chest and started crying too. I hadn't even wondered where her mother was all day. Just figured it was Skoby's turn to have her for Christmas. That happens in joint custody.

It could've been five minutes, or even fifteen that had past, with me and Krissi sitting in the middle of her library crying like two little orphans. But when we came up for air, all we could do was smile. This baby had healed me twice in thirty days. And the second healing wasn't even intentional.

"Well, that felt good!" I smiled, wiping my eyes. Krissi reached up and thumbed away a tear that I'd missed.

"Where's your mama. Jo?" She asked. "And not Mama Jo. Your mama that carried you in her belly."

How did she know the specifics of motherhood? Who had raised this little grown person?

"I don't know." I answered as honestly as I could. "But I hope she's okay wherever she is."

"I hope my mama's okay too." She said.

"Me too, Krissi." I added on a nod. "But you know who I care about most right now?" I widened my eyes, holding her little hands tight.

"Who!?" She chirped.

"Me and you!" I poked her chest with my finger, sending her into a laughing fit.

"I'm okay." She said after I poked her a few more times.

"Good." I said. "And so am I. Now let's go dance with Uncle Lem. I heard he was looking for two *ok* dancing partners!" I hopped up off the floor and Krissi did the same. We rushed down the hallway hand and hand until we reached the party room.

Skoby

She was perfect in every way that mattered. Anybody that would let Uncle Lem spin them around to *This Christmas* by Donny Hathaway was perfect in my sight, and she and Krissi were doing just that when I walked in from outside. I'd peeped in on the two of them hugged up in the library sharing a moment a few minutes prior, and decided that it was something that didn't need my attention. So, I left them to it and went on about my business.

Jo blended into the craziness that was my family like a piece we didn't know was missing. And it was so frustrating that she didn't know that. So fucked up that I might never get the courage or the chance to tell her. I wanted her the same way I'd wanted her since the night I brought her home with me. This was more than an infatuation. My ass had fallen in love.

I left the wall where I'd been chopping it up with Smitty, when Vanessa walked up and asked him to dance. Those two were an accident waiting to happen, but I wasn't putting my nose where it didn't belong. Jo and Krissi were wearing Uncle Lem out, and I knew if I didn't take the pressure off at least one of his arms, he was gonna be filing for workman's comp the following week. I approached the center of the floor where the trio was dancing, getting a wink and a nod from Gams on my way. It felt like junior prom when I asked the finest girl in my class, Stefanie, to dance. My heart was beating a hole in my damn chest. I walked slowly so I wouldn't slip and bust my ass like I did before I made it to Stefanie.

"Unc, you mind if I take one of these pretty ladies off your hands for a minute?" I asked, grinning at Jo.

"Go head. I think I done wore this one out!" Unc extended Jo's hand to me, and she didn't object, laughing at Uncle Lem as I easily pulled her away.

She looked so damn pretty in that bright green dress that hugged her curves and flared at the knee. That wild hair I loved was pulled into a slick ponytail at the back of her head. She'd had it straightened. It looked nice, but it was a direct contradiction of the fireball I knew she was.

Jo melted into my body with little to no resistance as BoyzIIMen sang *"Let it Snow"* over the sound system. I could've gone through the whole song without saying anything. The fact that she was letting me hold her was enough. It was all I'd really wanted for Christmas.

"Thanks for inviting me, Skoby. I had a really good time." She whispered in my ear. The warmth from her breath would've made my dick jump if I wasn't concentrating so hard on not letting that happen.

"No problem. Glad you enjoyed yourself." I whispered over the music, hoping that my mouth being so close to her neck was causing some kind of reaction too.

"It was Krissi's idea, you know? Inviting you over?" I added.

"I know." I felt her cheeks spreading into a smile against the side of my face.

"Skoby, have you um… talked to Krissi about her mama?"

"What you mean?" I asked, reaching in my pocket when my phone started vibrating.

"You know what, never mind. I just. I was—"

"Hold on. I gotta take this." I pressed at the small of Jo's back before releasing her and stepping away. "It's Krissi's mama. You ain't… you ain't psychic or nothin', huh?" I squinted, swiping right to answer the call.

"Boy no!" She laughed that high pitched laugh, eyes following me as I grabbed Krissi from Uncle Lem, and headed off to the living room so she could talk to her absentee mother.

"You okay, Mama?"

Instead of crying like a regular five-year-old or questioning where she was, Krissi was looking at her mother's face on the phone screen, asking if she was ok.

"Yeah. I'm… I'm okay, Ladybug." Kerri replied, eyes red from crying or lack of sleep, voice tired and strained from arguing with her people or partying all night. It was hard to tell the difference and harder to give a fuck.

"Did you get alotta stuff for Christmas, baby?" She asked.

"Yeah." Krissi said. "I mean *yes ma'am*." She corrected when I mouthed it to her from my seat beside her on the couch.

"You have such good manners, Krissi. I'm so proud of you!" Kerri smiled.

Krissi traced her pointer finger around her mama's face on the screen, and I could sense a million questions whirling in those pretty little eyes.

"Why didn't you come, Mama?" She asked in a tone that broke my heart.

But I wanted to know the answer just as much as Krissi did. I'd known Kerri long enough to know she'd throw out some bullshit. But I wasn't bailing her out this time. She needed to face the fucking music.

"Bug, I was... I couldn't, okay. I mean I planned to, but sometimes plans don't work out." She rushed through an answer. Then some loud nigga in the background took her attention from the phone.

"Ladybug, you know I love you right?" She said, widening her eyes at Krissi.

"Umm hmm." Krissi nodded her head.

"Good. Do you love me?" She asked, looking over her shoulder at whoever had entered the room before looking back at Krissi.

"Umm hmm." Krissi nodded again. "I gotta go, Mama." Krissi traced her finger around Kerri's face one more time. Then they both kissed the screen before Krissi ended the call and handed the phone back to me.

"Come on. Let's go finish dancing now, Daddy!" She hopped off the sofa, and extended her hand. I stood up and joined her and we headed back toward the party room.

Before we got there, we bumped into Jo re-entering the house with two small gift boxes in her hands.

"Hey, you leavin' already?" I asked.

"Don't go yet, Jo. Daddy needs a dance partner!" Krissi whined.

"Oh, no. I'm not leaving." Jo smiled, walking over to me and Krissi. "I just stepped out to grab these gifts. I left em in the car."

"Are they for me?" Krissi was way too hype about Christmas gifts. She'd already ripped over two dozen gifts open that morning. We'd overcompensated to fill the void of Kerri not being there.

"Yes." Jo nodded. "Well one of them is anyway. The other's for your daddy, if that's okay with you."

"*Okaaay.*" The girl had the nerve to poke out her lip after I'd purchased and assembled a mini-Mercedes coupe for her to ride up and down the driveway.

"I want the pink one!" Krissi yelled. Damn brat.

"Well it's a good thing I… I mean *Santa* put your name on that one!" Jo bit down on her lip, eyes scanning from me to Krissi.

"It's cool, she don't believe in Santa." I grinned, as Krissi took the gift from Jo's hand and flopped down on the floor to rip it open.

"Uncle Lemon said Santa Claus is a symbol of oppression." I was afraid she was gonna remember him saying that shit. And it was just my luck that she had.

"Please don't entertain that conversation." I pleaded to Jo. "It's a deep, dark alley that nobody wants to travel down."

"I don't know. I kinda like deep dark alleys!" She winked.

Was she flirting with me? She couldn't be flirting with me. Jo knew damn well the shit I'd do to her if she was.

"Jo, this book doesn't have any words in it. I think you got jipped!"

"Did she just say…?" Jo squinted at me.

"*Uncle Lem.*" I shrugged.

She shook her head and carefully sat down on the floor next to Krissi. It always amazed me how she never hesitated to literally get down to Krissi's level.

"This is a special kinda book, Krissi." Jo explained. "All the pages are blank. But you have to fill them up."

"With what?" Krissi's nose crinkled when she looked up at Jo.

"With *words*, silly!" Jo poked her nose. "And it came with this special pen." Jo pulled a matching pink ink pen with Krissi's named engraved in glittery letters, from a long slot along the spine of the book.

"What am I supposed to write?" Krissi grabbed the pen and flipped the book open to the first page.

"Whatever you want. It's a journal." Jo answered.

"Did you have a journal when you were little, Jo?" Krissi gripped the pen and slowly wrote her name at the top of the page with her tongue wagging for concentration purposes.

"Yep. I still do." Jo watched my baby girl spell her own name without asking for any help.

"What do you write about?" She looked up from her journal and asked.

I was so zoomed into their conversation that I'd forgotten I had a gift in my hand.

"Everything." Jo replied. "Happy stuff. Sad stuff. And sometimes mad stuff. That's what journals are for. They listen and they don't talk back…unless you ask them to."

"I like the sound of that!" Krissi's cheeks spread into a smile. "Can I write something about *you* in my journal?"

"Umm…sure. I guess. It's yours. You can write whatever you want."

"Ok. It's J-Owe, right?" Krissi asked, squinting at Jo.

"Actually, it's *Joletta*." Jo corrected to my surprise. "Jo's my nickname."

"Joletta's prettier. Can I call you Joletta?" She'd made it as far as the *O* before Jo said yes then spelled out the rest.

Krissi quickly advised us that her journal entry was a private matter and that we should move on with opening my gift while she finished writing in the library. And then came the awkwardness of being alone with Jo, wanting to say things that I knew that I shouldn't.

"So what's in my box?" I asked, breaking the silence after Krissi skipped off.

"I don't know. Open it." She smiled.

"Jo, come on. Just tell me."

"But what's the fun in that? Just open it!" She rushed me, smile almost as wide as her face.

I peeled the blue wrapping paper from the gift that was exactly the same size as Krissi's. It was no surprise that there was a journal inside. Red with a red pen to match. I'd never let on that I enjoyed reading or writing in my spare time, but apparently, Jo was up to something. That smile on her face had relaxed a bit, not taking away from her beauty at all.

"Thanks?" I squinted.

"Lose the question mark." She piped.

"No offense, but what am I supposed to do with this?"

"Did you not just hear me giving Krissi instructions?"

"I did. But I don't see how this is an appropriate gift. Krissi actually likes books and shit. I could do without em."

"It's not about a *like*. It's about a *need*." She returned, stepping in closer to me.

"And you think I need this, why?" I asked.

"For the same reason Krissi needs it. Hell, the same reason *I* need it."

"And that is?"

"Dammit Skoby, do I have to spell it out for you?" She threw her hands up.

"That might help." I looked her straight in the eye, daring her to spell out whatever she had on her chest.

"It's therapeutic." She said. "And here lately, it's been the only way to express how much I miss people."

"That's cool. But I don't need a journal for that."

"Fine." She dropped her hands at her side.

"Bet." I returned.

"*Cool.*" She snapped her neck.

"I'mma go back in here and… fuckit. I don't know."

"And I'll go check on Krissi. Cuz…yeah, whatever."

I turned to walk away, tryna figure out what exactly the fuck had just happened. It felt like an argument, but there was nothing to argue for. I'd just spazzed the fuck out over a leather-bound journal.

"Skoby, wait." Jo stopped me in my tracks right before I could stop myself.

I turned around to face her and I swear, every fucking twinkling light that Gams had lining the beams of my ceiling, had casted a glow down on Jo's skin that made me weak in the got damn knees.

"Wassup?" That wasn't at all indicative of the voice in my head that wanted to scream *Please fucking kiss me before I die!*

"Do you miss me?" She asked. And she may as well have asked me if my name was Skoby Twan Paul.

Because the answer was *yes*.

I miss you more than you will ever fucking know.

I miss the taste of your lips—the set on your face and the set between your legs.

I miss the warmth of your breath against my neck in the morning.

I miss that vanilla shit that emanates from your skin like some kinda magic potion.

And most of all, I miss that wild ass hair on your head, and the way it feels between my fingers.

But, "What kinda question is that?" is what I said instead.

"You pushed me outta your life. You're only here on some sympathy shit for Krissi. Now you tryna play me with a question like that? Shit's foul, Jo."

"So, I'll take that as a no. Tell everybody I said good night." She rushed toward the front door, to grab her coat and purse off the coat rack.

"Jo." I hurried up behind her. "Jo, wait!" I pulled at her wrist.

"I would *never* lie to Krissi!" Her eyes were glossed with tears. "Cause I know how that feels. I know how *she* feels. And you do too."

Her lips trembled and I couldn't take that shit.

"Look, I'm sorry, alright. I didn't mean that shit. I'm just… you just don't get it."

"Get what?"

"Get *this*!" I spread my arms out to either side of me.

"Do you know how hard it is to be around you? I'm out here laughin' and jokin' and shit, when ain't nothin' funny about the way I'm feelin'."

"And how's that?" She folded her arms across her chest, sending the peak of her cleavage up.

"Like I miss you." I replied with all honesty. I didn't have shit to lose.

Without a moment's notice, Jo had dropped her shit and was up on me, reaching up to grab both sides of my face and pulling my lips down into a kiss. Her tongue was so warm and soft against mine. She was basically taking me, and I sure as hell didn't mind.

"Wait, what're we doin'?" I pulled away to make sure I wasn't trippin'.

"Has it been that long since we kissed? Damn!"

It *had* been that long. And having gone without the sweetness of her lips for long enough, I released all inhibitions and accepted the invitation. But I couldn't let her do me like that—tryna take control like I hadn't brought her ass to climax the first night we met, using nothing but my finger. I pulled her in against me, dick hard against her belly. Then I swallowed her mouth up like she wanted me to, until I felt her body relax in my embrace.

"You think Krissi's asleep in there?" She sucked away from my tongue, glancing down at my shit before bringing her eyes back up to me.

"I can check. Why?" I asked.

She pulled her bottom lip between her teeth and glanced down at my dick again. I almost tore my fucking ACL running to that library to check on Krissi.

And she was out like a light, curled up in a pillow pin with her journal and pen in hand, and a thumb in her mouth.

"Five minutes." Jo said.

"Damn, thassit?"

"For now. You want this pussy or not?"

That question alone got her picked up off the floor and rushed up the stairs. We barely made it in the room before I unzipped the back of her dress and slid it down to the floor. I made quick work of getting outta my pants, before Jo stopped me with a hand to my chest.

"Wait." She gave a piercing stare, never breaking eye contact as she stepped out of her dress, leaving it puddled on the floor, quickly dropping to her knees in front of me. Jo was glowing with lust, lips plump and glossed as she looked up at me stroking my dick hard as fuck, only pulling away to spit on it before she went back to stroking it again.

"Jo, fuck!" I moaned as she took me into her hot mouth, massaging my balls and taking me deep down her throat.

My eyes fell closed, knees felt weak. Jo was bobbing on my shit like she'd been hungry for it. I was hesitant to grip the back of her head, but I wanted to so bad. Her mouth and throat were so wet and warm, I wanted to bury my dick in it as far as it would go. Then, as if she could sense my needs, maybe she tasted it on her tongue, she reached up and pulled my hand from my side, and placed it behind her head. I pushed in deeper, holding her head there until I felt like she needed to breathe. Jo gagged on my shit, wet noises seeping out as spit cascaded from the corners of her mouth. And she didn't bother cleaning it up, somehow knowing that that nasty shit turned me on. I fucked her face harder, looking down and watching her take me like a pro. She hummed on it, sending tiny vibrations from my head to the base of my shaft. I pulled my hand from behind her head as she slid her lips down to the tip, then used both hands to massage my shit in a twisting motion while flipping her wet tongue around my throbbing head.

"That feels so fuckin good, baby." I moaned, damn near out of breath.

"Umm hmm." She hummed with her mouth sheeting back over me, lowering one of her hands as she raised up on the pads of her feet, spread her legs wide and finger fucked her pussy.

She took me back down her throat in one swift slide. She was gagging, and slurping, and sucking me so hard, I couldn't stop the explosion if I wanted to.

Jo got up off the floor with a smile on her face, feeling like she'd won, sticking her tongue out to display the hot cum I'd just shot in her mouth. Shit sent my dick right back to rock solid before I knew it. Then she swallowed it, and I knew this mother fucker was tyna win.

"What you doin'!?" She smiled as I grabbed her at the waist. I turned her ass around, bent her over the dresser, and slid in that pussy before she could say another word.

"Fuck, Skoby!" She screamed so loud, I was thankful for the loud music playing all over the house.

"I missed you so fuckin' much!" I moaned. "Don't you ever take this pussy away from me!" I slammed into that chocolate love so hard that my thighs clapped her cheeks.

"I won't baby." She purred, squeezing tight around my dick. "Fuck me, Skoby. Put your thumb in my ass!"

And I did. Pulled the band off, and gripped a hand full of that wild hair that I'd missed so much, and pulled it with my thumb sliding deep into her ass hole. My nuts tingled at the sight of Jo's ass being thrown back at me with every thrust. I was so deep inside her, I could feel her next thought. With her head pulled back and moans swimming from her lips, I pumped into her faster till blood rushed to the tip of my dick.

"Dammit, Jo!" I screamed, filling her pussy with cum while she squirted and screamed. We breathed our way through it, both knowing that the shit had built up too long. I was never gonna be able to let this woman go, and there was nothing she could do or say to make me.

Jo had somehow convinced me that we should wash up and rejoin the festivities, when all I really wanted to do was fall asleep between her legs and wake up in the same spot. Gams and Uncle Lem had zoomed in on us coming down the stairs. And Smitty and Vanessa's messy asses were right alongside them instigating.

"What was y'all doin' up there?" Gams was the first to ask.

"Fuckin'!" Vanessa blurted, laughing hard as hell. She'd been hitting that eggnog hard.

"What *she* said." Uncle Lem added. "Went up there with a perm and came down with an afro. But that ain't my business. Y'all want some more eggnog? Somebody gotta drink my portion!"

"I'll do it! I'll drink your portion, Uncle Lem!" Vanessa raised her hand. Smitty put it back down. Those two had gotten way too familiar.

"It doesn't matter what we were doing. It matters what we're about to do." Jo broke in, holding my hand like she was scared I might run away. But she didn't have to worry. I never would.

"I'mma go grab Krissi." She whispered in my ear before kissing my cheek with the same set of lips that had just sucked my fucking soul a loose. "We'll meet you on the dance floor!" She spun away, giving me a perfect view of that ass. I was gonna fuck the shit outta her as soon as this damn company left.

Jo

The Christmas Soul Train line was a success. Me and Krissi brought down the house with our impromptu hip bump—a dance that had me dropping it low since Krissi's hip only came just above my knees. It was a good time. Probably the best time, if I'm being honest. Instead of sitting at home on the couch moping and crying about what I didn't have, I did what Mama would've wanted me to do, and spent the holidays with the *Fruit Man's* grandson.

174

It had seemed so far-fetched, falling in love with Skoby. We had so much in common, I thought our pain might push us apart.

But it didn't.

Instead it acted as a magnet, pulling our hearts together and teaching us *how to love* even in brokenness.

"I love you, Skoby." I whispered in his ear, arms wrapped around his neck after the house had cleared and we had the party room to ourselves. I wasn't sure what his response would be, and really didn't care. I knew exactly what I was feeling and I'd shared my truth. And no matter what, I wouldn't be taking it back.

"I love you too, Joletta." He whispered back, big hands resting at the rise of my hips. And I won't front, I was relieved.

"Seriously?" I leaned back and glared at him playfully. "We goin' down this road again?"

"What? You let Krissi say it." He whined. This *grown man whined!*

"I got a two person maximum on that name." I said. "My daddy and Krissi. Thassit."

"What if it slips out while I'm in that pussy?"

"Skoby!"

"Or while my thumb's in your butt?"

"Don't play with me."

"I'm just sayin. Shit happens in the heat of the moment. I can't help that. What you gone do, tell me to stop?"

"I ain't say all that…" I rolled my eyes and backed away.

Then he chased me up the stairs to the room where it had all started.

And yes, this was going in my journal!

The end...

More stories by Sabrina
Lena
Yours Truly… Or Something Like That (Book One)
Yours Truly… Lost And Found (Book Two)
Bodies: Secrets, Flesh, & Blood (Book One)
Bodies: Black & Blue (Book Two)
Bodies: Carried Away (Book Three)
No Love (A Story Of Love Avoided)
The Lake (A Novelette)
So This Is Christmas? (A Novel)
Butterflies In A Mason Jar
Shaw Siblings After-Words: Keys And Choruses-Jordyn & Russell (Book One)
Shaw Siblings After-Words: Addicted-Jessie & Chloe (Book Two)
Shaw Siblings After-Words: Separated-Josh & Simone (Book Three)
A Scattered Life Series: Six Marble Headstones (Book One)
The Bricks: Apt. B17 Camille (Book One)
The Bricks: Apt. F53 Tasia (Book Two)
The Bricks: Apt. F58 Keshia (Book Three)
The Bricks: Apt. A1 Freddie (Book Four)
A Collection Of Christmas Stories From The Bricks
Stone Bodies Productions: The Grind (Book One)
Stone Bodies Productions: The Fall (Book Two)
Petals
The Color Spectrum Duet: Ivory (Book One)
The Color Spectrum: Ebony (Book Two)
By Chencia C. Higgins

To the readers…
Thank you so much for taking the time to read this story.
I hope you enjoyed reading it as much as I enjoyed writing it!
For more of my stories, please visit my author page
On Amazon.com @ Sabrina B. Scales.
And please, rate and review.
It's the best gift any reader can leave for an author,
worth more than its weight in gold!
For inquiries, please contact me at:
SabrinaBScales@gmail.com
or
On Facebook Author Sabrina B. Scales
or
On Instagram @AuhtorSabrinaBScales
Or
www.sabrinabscales.com
Thanks a bunch. Keep reading!

CPSIA information can be obtained
at www.ICGtesting.com
Printed in the USA
LVHW051949171220
674450LV00014B/1455